I0817783

Southern Haunts

A MAX PORTER PARANORMAL-MYSTERY

Stuart Jaffe

Southern Haunts is a work of fiction. Names, characters, places, and incidents either are the product of the author's imagination or are used fictitiously, and any resemblance to any persons, living or dead, business establishments, events, or locales is entirely coincidental.

SOUTHERN HAUNTS

Cover art by Jeff Dekal

ISBN 13: 978-1-7337308-7-7

First Edition: December, 2015
First Hardcover Edition: January, 2024

For Benjamin and Zachary

when you're old enough to read this series,
I hope you enjoy it

Also by Stuart Jaffe

Max Porter Paranormal Mysteries

Southern Bound
Southern Charm
Southern Belle
Southern Gothic
Southern Haunts
Southern Curses
Southern Rites
Southern Craft
Southern Spirit
Southern Flames
Southern Fury
Southern Souls
Southern Blood
Southern Graves
Southern Dead
Southern Hexes
Southern Hart

Nathan K Thrillers

Immortal Killers
Killing Machine
The Cardinal
Yukon Massacre
The First Battle
Immortal Darkness
A Spy for Eternity
Prisoner
Desert Takedown
Lone Star Standoff
The Puppeteer
Blowback
Prime

The Ridnight Mysteries

The Water Blade
The Waters of Taladoro
Waterfire

The Parallel Society

The Infinity Caverns
Book on the Isle
Rift Angel
Lost Time
Pages of Glass
The Bold Warrior
City of Infinity

The Malja Chronicles

The Way of the Black Beast
The Way of the Sword and Gun
The Way of the Brother Gods
The Way of the Blade
The Way of the Power
The Way of the Soul

Gillian Boone novels

A Glimpse of Her Soul
Pathway to Spirit

Stand Alone Novels

After The Crash
Real Magic
Founders

Short Story Collection

10 Bits of My Brain
10 More Bits of My Brain
The Bluesman
The Marshall Drummond Case Files: Cabinet 1
The Marshall Drummond Case Files: Cabinet 2
The Marshall Drummond Case Files: Cabinet 3

Non-Fiction

How to Write Magical Words: A Writer's Companion
For more information, please visit ***www.stuartjaffe.com***

Southern Haunts

Chapter 1

DAY ONE

MAX PORTER WAITED FOR HIS NAME to be called so he could have the honor of overpaying for coffee and bagels. Not long ago, he would have seriously considered it an honor. He and Sandra had been living in a trailer, unsure of when they would be dead broke. But after successfully handling a job for Cecily Hull, the Porters had more money than ever — enough to have bought a new home in the upper-middle-class housing developments surrounding Wake Forest University, and enough to rent a second floor office in the less posh section of downtown Winston-Salem.

The little coffee shop on the corner of Liberty and 6th smelled comfortable, and every morning that Max strolled in for a quick breakfast reminded him that such comfort could not be enjoyed by everyone. Losing almost everything certainly filled him with greater appreciation for what he had. And that even included Drummond.

"Morning, Max. Getting your usual crap, I see." Marshall Drummond, the ghost of a 1940s detective and the only ghost Max could see, had a personality that required patience and subtle appreciation. He floated next to the barista and snarled at each coffee concoction handed out. "A cup o' joe should be a cup o' joe. A little sugar or cream, if you have to, but this is ridiculous." The man always appeared as he had when he died — classic 1940s detective, with a beaten Fedora, a long coat, and plenty of attitude. Despite decades of observation, he accepted little of the changing ways of the world. Still, Max valued him greatly.

Heck, I'd probably be dead if not for the old, dead guy.

"How's Sandra?" Drummond asked, lowering his voice as if those around him could actually hear a word he said.

"The same," Max said under his breath. After the initial weeks of having money again, of not worrying if they wanted to eat ice cream, see a movie, or buy overpriced coffee, the euphoria had worn off. Then they bought the house and rented the office and another joyous wave splashed over them. But as the months crept onward, Sandra had become distant — not just to Max; Drummond had noticed, too.

"Maxine Poster," the barista called out.

In one hand, Max balanced the cardboard carrier with two coffees and three bagels and paid with his other hand. Once outside, he headed across 6th, away from the bus station, police department, and courthouse. His office was just up from the coffee shop on Liberty, but Drummond said nothing. Max had been taking this detour for a few weeks now.

"Look," Drummond said, "I don't mean to be a nag, but you've got to do something. Sandra's got a problem."

Max shook his head. "You've never really understood marriage. We're just in a down swing, that's all. Every marriage goes through it. There are ups and downs. Times you're really close and times you hardly speak. Nothing has to be wrong for it to happen. It's like a natural cycle."

"More like a rollercoaster."

"You can't press these things. If there's a problem, she'll tell me when she's ready. Until then, I've got to trust that whatever it is, if there's anything at all, it isn't going to harm us. We've gotten past the idea of keeping secrets to protect each other."

"You better be right. I can't abide anything happening to that sweet gal."

"You and me both. Go check on her, if it'll make you feel better. Let her know I'll be right up with breakfast."

"Sure thing. You're going to see the kid, right?"

"Yeah. If he's still around."

As Max turned the corner, Drummond disappeared. Max pressed on, crossing the parking lot behind the Liberty Street buildings and heading north. Soon, the parking lots ended and a long stretch of dilapidated buildings took over for a few blocks. Max had no idea what they had been — Sandra had told him she saw several ghosts dressed like warehouse laborers in the area — but he knew if it ever mattered, he could find out with ease. Years of researching Winston-Salem had its benefits. What did matter, however, was the kid living under a tarp stretched off the remains of a brick wall.

The kid went by PB. He wouldn't say what it stood for, so Max called him Peanut Butter, but Drummond continued to call him *Kid*. He looked about fourteen, kept his hair buzzed short, and often had the long distance stare of a combat veteran. Max had first met him when PB was begging for change outside the coffee shop. Something about this young man struck Max, and he followed PB to this squat. Since then, every few days, Max brought him a bagel or some other food.

"Hey, Ghostman," PB said as Max approached. He had once caught Max talking with Drummond, and when Max said he spoke with a ghost, PB laughed and gave him the name.

Max handed over one of the bagels. As PB stretched out from under the tarp, Max noticed a bruise darkening the boy's eye. "You got trouble?"

"I'm living on the streets. I always got trouble. How about you? You getting laid yet?"

"Excuse me? I get laid plenty."

"Sure you do. Every married couple going through a fight always keeps having sex."

Max looked in the boy's bruised eyes, trying to figure out why PB tried to pick a fight. Only problem — he wasn't wrong. Max and Sandra hadn't slept together in three weeks. Sex and money — the two deadliest issues in any marriage. Whenever things went downhill, sex disappeared first. If they start fighting about money, Max knew they had hit rock bottom.

"We're not going to talk about my sex life."

"Whatever," PB said around a chunk of bagel.

"That shiner looks fresh. You need any help?"

"From you? What are you gonna do, huh? Call your pet

ghost to fight?"

From behind, a sleazy voice call out. "Well, well. Is this the famous Ghostman?"

PB's eyes bugged out as he stashed the half-eaten bagel in his shirt. Three men sauntered up. They were an odd bunch — tough, clearly, but dressed like slime from the 70s. The leader stood in the middle with a brown, leather jacket draped over one shoulder and a toothpick jutting from the corner of his mouth. His two muscular buddies each sported aviator shades.

The leader set one foot atop a pile of rubble and leaned his elbow on his knee. "Is that you, man? You the guy Punching Bag here says can see ghosts?"

Punching Bag? PB? Max glanced down and PB shied back. To the leader, Max said, "Who're you?"

"I'm the one in charge of these blocks. Nothing goes on around here without my saying it does. I see everything and I protect this turf. That's why I'm called the Wolf."

Max chuckled. "The Wolf of Winston-Salem."

"That's right," the leader said, as his two men spread out in opposite directions. "And you better show some respect or we'll turn you into a punching bag, too."

A few years ago, Max would have been confused by the situation. He would have still seen the danger, but he would have missed the subtler aspects of Wolf's behavior — the darting eyes, the constant chewing of the toothpick, the excess bravado in his body posture. Years of hard-earned experience informed Max that this guy did not own the block as he claimed. More likely, Wolf had been making a play to take over the area. That's why he was beating up the runaways like PB. He started on the bottom and hoped to either gain the notice of those higher up, or he would simply have to take it all by force.

Max had no clue who those higher ups were or what they valued in this particular block, but his mind leaned toward the most obvious — drugs. That seemed to fit. Wolf was a low-level drug dealer who wanted to expand his territory and gain some power. Unless the other possibility proved true.

"Amateurs," Max muttered.

"What now? Ghostman's got something stupid to say?"

"I've always got something to say. Stupid or otherwise. I was just trying to figure out why you think beating me up would help you at all. I'm not a druggie and I don't come around here other than to give PB a hand once-in-a-while. Beating me up won't send a message to anybody because I'm not connected with anyone you want to send a message to."

Wolf's lips pulled back to show a gold tooth. "Who said anything about sending a message? Maybe I just want to beat on some rich prick."

That was the other possibility. Wolf led a gang of three that were as lost and hopeless as PB. They simply scrounged around the area to survive and took out their aggressions on the nearest target.

Hard to believe that only a block over, the civilized world existed.

"Only one thing can save you, Ghostman. You know that, right?"

"What's that?"

"Ain't it obvious? We want to see some ghosts. PB told us all about it, so we want to see you in action."

Max didn't need to look at PB to know shame blushed across the boy's face. "I don't know why you'd believe such a thing. I can't summon a ghost. I only —"

"That's not good for you. Or PB. I don't like being lied to."

Max set his coffee carrier down. "Let's get something clear here. You don't give a crap about me or ghosts or anything like that. You want an excuse to fight."

"Oh, I see. We got a smart guy here."

"Problem for you is that you're a weakling."

"What did you say?"

"You heard me. That's why you got these two muscleheads with you. You're afraid to fight on your own." Max made sure to lock eyes with each of Wolf's wingmen. "You do know that he's using you, right? I mean, I hope at some point, he's really shown you that he's tough enough. Otherwise, either one of you could beat him to a pulp and take over. Though I don't know why you'd want this crappy block, but that's your business."

Wolf must have seen the doubt creeping into his men. He jutted a finger at Max. "You shut up. You can't talk yourself out of this. And I don't need these guys to destroy you."

As Wolf tossed his jacket aside, Max stepped forward. He figured he wouldn't be getting out of this with ease, so at least this way, he only had to fight one guy. He had a chance.

Wolf jumped toward Max with a fist pulled back. Max cinched up his shoulder, deflecting the punch from his face. With Wolf standing over him, he had the perfect position to throw an elbow to the gut. He followed with two kicks to the shins and a crack on the side of the head.

"Whoa, there, Max." Drummond appeared behind PB. "What're you pounding on some kids for?"

"Look around you," Max spat out.

PB's eyes widened. "He's doing it. He's talking to a ghost."

Wolf's men started at the accusation. Despite their shades, Max could tell they were looking in every direction as if a ghost would suddenly appear.

"Little gang thing going here," Drummond said. "Need any help?"

Max shook his head. He picked up the coffee carrier and headed toward the street. One of the muscleheads stepped toward Max, but Drummond passed a chilling hand across the guy's back. That stopped him. Instead of pursuing Max, he rushed to Wolf's aid, and the three hurried off. Max looked for PB, but he had slipped away.

Probably for the best.

Drummond floated up beside Max. "Boy, I leave you alone for a few minutes and you start taking on the whole city."

"I don't know what that was all about. Maybe just punks fighting for their little bit, but I don't know."

"Maybe you should give PB a little distance for now."

"Maybe."

"Well then, I got the perfect thing for you."

Max arched an eyebrow. “Oh?”

“That’s why I came to fetch you. We got new clients waiting in the office. Looks like a ghost is trying to hurt a woman’s baby.”

“Oh.”

Chapter 2

FOR MAX, TALES OF GHOSTS, WITCHES, AND CURSES no longer held the same sense of fear, foreboding, or intrigue they once held. He had heard more than he cared to consider and had experienced more than he dared to remember. Besides, if he really wanted to get in touch with the supernatural, he simply had to talk with Drummond. If that wasn't enough, he could ask his wife to list all the dead people hanging around. Sandra saw ghosts with ease.

So, Max did not relish the prospect of sitting through another tear-filled telling of frightening loud noises or terrifying spectral images. At the same time, he knew he would listen. If he couldn't help PB, then maybe he could do some good for somebody.

As Max and Drummond entered the office, he saw Sandra sitting behind his wide desk with a white man and a black woman waiting. The office was a wonderful mix of the old and the new. The building itself dated back to the 1960s — closer to Drummond's world than any other space they had considered — with a long bank of windows, generous ceilings, and old moldings around the doors. The interior, however, was completely modern — still smelling of new carpeting and new computers.

Before Max could open his mouth, the man approached with his hand extended. "Hi, I'm Wayne Darian. This is my wife Shawnee." Shawnee remained seated with her hands folded atop her pregnant belly. "Thank you so much for taking our case."

"Hold on, there," Max said. "I haven't even heard what you

want, yet."

"Right. Of course. Well, then, thank you for taking the time to listen."

Max glanced at Sandra. She shot back a look that said *I don't know what they want either.* He pulled up a chair next to his wife. "Let's start at the beginning."

Wayne nodded, rubbing his hands against his legs as he settled back down. "Sure, the beginning."

Drummond floated across the room toward the far wall — the one with the built-in bookshelf. It had been the deciding feature. Drummond had spent so many decades living in the bookshelf of their old office that Max thought it might be easier to transition to a new office with a familiar setting. Also, Max made sure to place a few false books filled with whiskey bottles inside. Drummond couldn't drink them but liked having them around.

"Did they say anything before we got back?" Drummond asked.

Max did his best to blot out Drummond's voice — a talent he had increased every day. "Please, Mr. Darian, what's this all about?"

Shawnee placed a tissue to her eyes and sniffled. "It's about our baby. Something's trying to get our baby."

"Something?"

"Please," Wayne said. "We know you two are involved with the supernatural." His face screwed up as if the word tasted bitter in his mouth.

Sandra put her hand out to Shawnee. "I know you're both upset. I can see that. If we can help, then we will. You've been calm and fine while we waited for Max. He's here now. Let's all stay calm and find out what's going on. Okay?"

Shawnee nodded. "Sorry, but this is all very foreign for us." She spoke with a Deep South drawl. Max had learned that the Southern drawl had many distinct variations depending on the area the speaker came from. He didn't know the differences well enough yet to pinpoint locations, but he knew enough to say that Shawnee was not from the Carolinas nor anywhere north.

Max put on a smile. "Why don't we start with you two? How did you meet? What brought you to Winston-Salem?"

Wayne and Shawnee held hands as they eased into a better memory. Wayne said, "I'm from Philly. Born and raised. Did my undergrad at Temple and went across to Princeton for my Masters. Library sciences. I work over in High Point. Not a bad commute from here."

"Librarians are some of my favorite people — considering all the research I do." To Shawnee, Max added, "And what about you?"

"Oh, I come from Alabama. Raised on the straight and narrow. I met Wayne at Princeton while I was in Med School. We moved here because of me. I got work at Wake Forest Baptist Hospital. It's just up the road from our house." Her voice cracked on the word *house.*

"Something wrong with the house?"

Wayne took over. "We were fine for the first year or so. Things only began happening in the last few months. It started when Shawnee began having these vivid, horrible dreams."

"I kept dreaming of my baby," Shawnee said. "I'd see it born on the kitchen table and there'd be all these creatures hanging over me, laughing, and biting the air around me, and they would grab for the baby. I'd scream but no sound would come out."

"She'd wake up in a cold sweat, and it would take hours for her to come down from the fear. At first, we thought it was just the hormones and worry of being pregnant. You know, like a reaction."

"But then I started seeing shadows moving out of the corner of my eye. Too many to be dismissed. I've heard noises, too. Old music and laughter and moaning. Whatever is in that house doesn't bother Wayne. Only me. That's why I think it wants my baby. I mean, isn't that what ghosts want? A young life."

Max pulled out his notepad and jotted a few keywords. "If your house is haunted and threatening your unborn child, why are you staying there?"

Wayne let go of Shawnee's hand and leaned forward. "We can't afford to move. Malpractice insurance and school bills alone are like a second mortgage. Plus we used what we had on the down payment for this house. I mean, I'm not crazy. If we can't fix this, we'll leave. But if there's a way to solve our problem without forcing us into even worse debt, we'll take that option. We like it here. We like our house — other than the obvious."

Sandra said, "Please, tell my husband about the other team you hired."

"Other team?" Max didn't like the sound of that.

Wayne bit at his thumbnail. "Like we said, this started a few months ago. I'm not going to be some movie husband that ignores his wife until the walls start bleeding. Once Shawnee's dreams went beyond just dreams, once she started seeing things in the house, we started looking for paranormal investigators."

"And these paranormal investigators didn't help?"

"They've done plenty. They said that our house has definitely got something inside it — a ghost, I guess. But the head of the team, Libby Broward, she said that she needed help, that whatever is after us goes beyond her team's capabilities."

"I see. So, she suggested you hire us."

"No. She's never heard of you. In fact, she wants to check you out before we agree to hire you."

Drummond leaned toward his coat pocket and whispered. Max often forgot that the damaged soul of a former ghost hunter, Leed, resided in Drummond's pocket. In fact, Max only noticed when he would catch Drummond talking with Leed. Something about that little blob of soul unsettled Max — far more than ghosts, witches, and curses ever had.

Drummond gave Max a quick nod. "You know this sounds fishy, right? I mean, Leed says this Broward lady is probably legit — if she were running a scam, she wouldn't suggest getting outside help — but the fact that she never heard of us seems wrong."

"That's okay," Max said to Wayne. "We're not the most visible group in this field."

"That may be," Drummond said, "but I still think it's fishy."

Sandra gestured toward Wayne — a subtle enough motion to quiet Drummond down. "Perhaps you could explain how you found out about us?"

"Oh, that came from a fellow librarian — Leon Moore."

Max bristled. Leon worked at the Z. Smith Reynolds Library at Wake Forest University — Max's favorite place to do research. Leon had spent many hours spying on Max for the Magi Group, an organization devoted to fighting the Hulls and anybody else who abused magic. Though Max was happy to have others fighting the Hulls alongside him, his experience with the Magi Group left a bitter taste. He didn't trust them. If for no other reason than the fact that they used magic, too.

"Ditch this case," Drummond said. "It's got nothing good surrounding it. And these two are really holding back. I don't like that."

Max had to agree. He felt bad for Shawnee. Nobody wanted to face a ghost attack, especially pregnant, but this all felt a little off like a painting slightly askew. Leon Moore's involvement, even tangential involvement, meant that this could be trouble.

Placing his fingertips on his desk, Max said, "Mr. and Mrs. Darian, I think this case —"

"— is perfect for us," Sandra said. "We'll take it."

Shawnee released a tense sigh. "Really?" She looked at her belly. "Thank you."

Max shot Sandra a sharp look but she kept her eyes on Shawnee. Wayne cleared his throat with a bashful face. "Ms. Broward still wants to meet you before this goes any further. We don't mean to offend you. It's just that, well, as she said it, there are a lot of frauds in this line of work, and because our problem is real, she doesn't want us getting hurt."

"We understand perfectly," Sandra said. "Let's meet her as soon as possible and then see the house."

"How about later today?"

"Great. Have her call us."

"Oh, thank you." Wayne hesitated. "Um, what about your fee?"

"Let's see what we're dealing with first. Then we can give you a fair estimate."

Wayne and Shawnee offered more thanks as they left the office. When Sandra closed the door behind them, she faced Max and Drummond staring at her. She put a defiant hand on her hip and set her jaw. "What?"

Neither said a word in response.

Chapter 3

MAX KNEW BETTER than to pick a fight with Sandra. She obviously wanted this case. Besides, he had made unilateral decisions for them before, so he had no ground to stand on.

They spent the rest of the morning quietly going through the paperwork of running a small business. It amazed Max how many forms they had to fill out and papers they had to file. Even with computers, the busywork never seemed to lessen. Having to be creative in their descriptions and explanations only slowed the process more. Each case had to be reclassified in order to be palatable to those in government who would balk at the idea of dealing with the supernatural as a business expense. By the time lunch arrived, Max was anxious to meet Liberty Broward just so he could get away from filling out government forms.

They met at Mr. Barbecue on Peters Creek Parkway, not too far south of the city. Max had to give Ms. Broward points for choosing a Lexington BBQ place. Max, Sandra, and Drummond entered the restaurant which was adorned with a long counter right at the front. Seating was off to either side.

A tall Japanese woman wearing a blue business outfit waved at them from the back corner. Seated with her was a chubby man with a thick beard and thicker glasses. Max and Sandra waved back, ordered their food, and walked over.

"Liberty Broward?" Max asked.

"Call me Libby," the woman said, offering her hand. "This is Jack Deere, my audio man."

Jack did a half-wave, half-salute without getting up.

Drummond crossed his arms. "Well, ain't they a piece of

work."

"Please," Libby said, "have a seat. I have a few questions for you before I offer up any of the case. I'm sure you understand."

"Shouldn't we wait for Wayne and Shawnee?" Max asked.

"They won't be joining us. This is not something they need to be bothered with. I think we can all agree they have enough to contend with."

Drummond gestured toward Libby, and Max needed nothing more. He could tell on his own that Libby forced her friendly attitude because her clients had forced her into this situation. Sandra noticed, too, but she seemed unwilling to react to it.

Libby had a pile of papers and folders which she neatly placed to the side. Clasping her hands together so that her bracelets jingled against the table, she pursed her lips and nodded. "As I understand things, the Darians have requested your aid, but they are willing to let me make the final decision on whether or not to include you."

Max wanted to bite into his sandwich, but instead he forced a smile of his own. "Look, we're not trying to steal your business. They came to us, and we want to help. That's all."

"I hope so. Let's start with a simple test. I want you to prove to me that you really do see ghosts."

"I thought you didn't know anything about us?"

Drummond clapped his hands once and pointed at Libby. "See. I told you not to trust her."

Libby gave her bracelets a single shake. "I do my research, too. When the Darians first mentioned you, I didn't know your names. But you've helped out a few people with their ghost problems, and that kind of thing gets noticed in certain circles. It wasn't too hard to find out a little about you. Unfortunately, what I have learned isn't enough to prove whether you're frauds or not."

"Frauds?"

Sandra put a hand on Max's arm. "She's just being cautious."

Libby went on, "My client is my top concern — not your egos. There is a serious problem going on at that house and it threatens that family. I won't let just anybody who claims they can see ghosts to jump in and start mucking about. This has to be handled professionally."

"Of course," Sandra said. "How do you want to test us?"

Libby held Sandra's gaze for a moment before frowning. She turned to Max. "I was told you were the one who sees ghosts, but your wife seems to be the one ready for the challenge."

"I only see one ghost," Max said. "But he'll tell me whatever you want to know."

Drummond chuckled. "Only if you're nice to me."

Libby returned her attention to Sandra. "There is a ghost in here that I want you to identify."

Sandra didn't bother to move her head. "There are many ghosts in here. Public places often have quite a few."

"Yes, but this one is connected to me."

With a slight shift, Sandra let her eyes roam across the dining area. "There's only one Japanese ghost in here. Would that be who you are looking for?"

"Any fraud would take one look at me and guess that the ghost should be Japanese. You'll have to do better."

"He's wearing slacks and a straw hat — like a porkpie — and when we entered he was swirling around the kitchen. Since then, he's taken notice of you and comes back every so often to watch you."

Max could tell Sandra had passed the test with her details, but he wanted Libby to know that he wasn't a fraud either — not because of ego, but because they needed to establish some trust in order to work together. "Drummond, do me a favor and ask this Japanese gentleman for his name."

"You got it," Drummond said.

A moment later, Max told Libby the ghost was her Uncle Yosh. Libby dashed a tear from her eye. "That's him. He loved the food here — not just this restaurant but all Southern food. Okay, you both are legit. Let's get started on the case."

Her audio man nudged the stuffed folder back in front of her. She opened it, turned a few pages, flipped a few photos, and stopped on a typed paper with the clear heading CASE REPORT.

"The client came to us three weeks ago complaining of unusual experiences in their house. Dreams that often repeated. Shadows moving just out of sight. And noises. Music playing where it couldn't be." Libby went on to cover their interviews with the Darians which matched the information Max and Sandra had received.

"We already know this," Max said.

Libby gripped her files tight and held her mouth even tighter. "Continuing on, I have a detailed list of questions we prepared for the presence in the house based on our hypothesis."

"Excuse me," Max said. Sandra put a hand on his arm, but he bolstered on. "What exactly is your hypothesis?"

Libby glared at Max. "I'm not about to give you everything we've worked hard to achieve. You are here to help us, not the other way around."

"Well, if you think we're going to be filling out reports for your file, you're crazy."

"I wouldn't dream of asking for you to behave professionally."

"Hey, we're plenty professional. But we're not ghost hunters playing at finding out about the supernatural and hoping to get picked up for some reality TV show. This world goes so far beyond ghosts, you have no idea."

"We care about our clients. We're not trying to get a TV deal or anything like that."

"You're poking a stick at a lion and you think all this paperwork and *professionalism* is going to shield you, but you're wrong. So, instead of testing us, maybe you should take the backseat and let us lead."

Sandra waved her hand between them. "That's enough."

"Aw," Drummond said. "Don't stop them. That was fun to watch."

"Max, it doesn't matter who is in charge. We've been hired to come in and use our unique skills to save a pregnant woman, and that's what we will do." Sandra lowered her voice and spoke in a sharp, deliberate pace. "You, too, Libby — the Darians hired us to come in and use our unique skills to help them, and that's what we will do. Understand?"

Libby bristled as she packed away her papers. "Fine. But you should know that I take this very seriously. If you do the slightest thing to jeopardize what we have accomplished to this point, I won't hesitate to do all I can to pull you off this case."

"Fair enough."

With a sheepish grin, Jack Deere flicked some earbuds across the table. "Man, you guys are so intense; you're going to go nuts over this. Check out what we recorded last night."

Max and Sandra tentatively picked up the earbuds and listened in. Jack tapped on his smartphone for a moment. "What you're about to hear was an EVP recorded around two-in-the-morning."

"EVP?"

Libby subtly rolled her eyes. "Electronic Voice Phenomenon. The best is Class A which requires no editing or enhancement."

"Very rare," Jack said growing more excited as he spoke. "Class B has some enhancements and might include discrepancies that are open to interpretation. Class C means heavier editing and thus, more discrepancy."

"Anything beyond that is too questionable for our standards."

"This recording we made last night needed only one gentle filter pass to take out some of the extraneous noise. This is Class B bordering on Class A. It's freaking incredible."

Max felt a nervous edge cross his skin as he covered his ears in order to hear better. He had fought witches — both dead and alive — knew a ghost and had dealt with magic on numerous occasions. Yet eavesdropping on the dead triggered an uneasiness in his stomach.

It was as if he was a kid watching a horror movie late at

night, and somehow he both knew and was oblivious to the approaching steps of his mother. If she dared to utter a sound, he would hit the ceiling with a churlish scream. But she wouldn't. This existed in his head, and she would forever be approaching.

Finally, Jack pressed his phone's screen, and Max could hear the sound of Libby's recorded voice.

LIBBY (tired): What is it?
JACK: Camera 2 is picking up something.
LIBBY: Carl? You got anything?"
CARL: Nothing.
JACK:Shh. Everybody shut up.

The group became still. Max could hear soft breathing. He pressed his ears tighter. He thought he heard a ticking clock.

The music that blared full-volume caused him to jump out of his seat. Sandra startled, too. A roaring blast of trumpets and trombones. A rowdy, big number that screamed of the 1920s. As Max's heart settled back down his throat, he could practically hear the flappers doing the Charleston.

The song lasted no more than ten seconds. After that, silence.

Stunned, Max and Sandra removed their earbuds. Libby flicked back her hair with a bit of triumph. "You see? This is serious."

Wide-eyed, Jack continued, "We've never recorded something like that before. I mean we have voices, but they're barely audible. This — man, you would've thought the band was right in that room."

"And that means that whatever is attacking Mrs. Darian, it is strong and determined. A moment ago, Mr. Porter, you asked for my hypothesis. I've changed my mind. I will tell you because I want you to grasp how dangerous this situation is."

Max did his best to hold back any sarcasm from his voice. "Please do."

"I think a woman died in that house during a party in the

1920s. I think that woman was pregnant. And I think she's angered and confused by Shawnee Darian's pregnancy. If we can get this ghost to realize she's dead and that it's okay for Shawnee to have a baby in the house, we might be able to get the dead woman to move on and stop haunting our client."

"We understand," Sandra said.

"I don't think you really do. A case like this could take quite some time to finish. That's the final part of the commitment I'm looking for from you two. I don't want you promising Shawnee your help, dropping in the house, talking with the spirits for a little, and then leave declaring everything fixed. None of this will be done until Shawnee's baby is born. Even after that, we might need to do regular follow-ups to make sure nothing starts up again. Are you prepared to help the Darians through this whole ordeal? Until the very end of it?"

"You have my word," Sandra said.

Drummond shrugged. "Why not? I ain't going anywhere."

Libby looked to Jack for a moment. If they communicated anything in that look, Max couldn't tell. But then Libby turned back. "Okay. The house is close by. Elizabeth Street — just up the road and off Academy. You can follow us. Carl, our videographer on the team, he's already there." From beneath the table, she pulled out a briefcase and stuffed her files inside. "We'll show you everything. Let's go."

Chapter 4

WHEN MAX HAD TURNED TEN YEARS OLD, he learned to roll with whatever the day brought. His special day began with the death of the family collie, Blondie, followed up with three hours caught in traffic, and ended with him being a half-hour late to his own party. As miserable as he felt at that moment, all his friends were waiting, and the party was a blast. Particularly because it ended with his first kiss — Sarah Wain.

The current day had started bad and only grew worse by the minute. He would push on, though. Perhaps the day would end on a better note. As they drove along Elizabeth Street, however, Max didn't feel so confident.

It was a quiet neighborhood lined with old houses pressed in close. The road traveled up and down short, steep hills, and the pavement needed work. Old maples stretched their branches overhead.

Everything about the area pointed to a lovely place to settle down. It chilled Max's skin to think about what really went on behind the closed doors. He had seen enough of the city's underbelly — the witches alone could cause nightmares. But here he would have to deal with a haunting. Despite how nonchalant he had felt when the Darians presented themselves at the office, approaching the house awakened his nerves.

Max saw Libby's car pull into the drive of an aqua-blue home with white trim and an American flag posted from the porch. He parked across the street. They were near the bottom of a downward slope which staggered the homes on a series of landings like steps. Cracks lined the concrete sidewalks.

Drummond stood by the car and stared at the house. "This

is the big, scary house? We've seen far worse."

"Yeah," Max said. "Maybe that's what bothers me."

Libby and Jack met them on the porch and ushered them in. The door opened to a living room with stairs on the left leading to the second floor. The walls were baby blue. A tattered sofa had been parked beneath the window and faced a large, wall-mounted flatscreen. A chipped coffee table sat between them, covered in newspapers as well as a shoebox. The air smelled of dog.

"Charming," Drummond said as if could still smell.

In one corner, a video camera sat on a tripod. Behind the camera, a man waved. Jack lifted his chin in acknowledgment as he cruised by on his way to the kitchen.

Libby placed a hand on her hip. "Carl. I didn't notice any holes outside. Did you bury the stones like I asked?"

Carl stepped from behind the camera. Max saw right away that Carl was a man at odds with himself. His thick, bottom lip protruded in a permanent pout and his clothing — ratty jeans and an orange t-shirt half-tucked-in — made him seem like a petulant fool. However, his face and hair were groomed with impeccable care. He spoke with a thick, wet voice that sounded dull-witted, yet his eyes sparkled with intelligence.

"Sorry, Ms. Broward. I haven't got to it yet." Carl did not look sorry at all. "I figured it was more important that I maintain the equipment. Right? What's the point, if we fail to capture any evidence because the cameras don't work properly when we need them to?"

"Your main focus is the cameras, but your job is to help us in our investigations. That means in every way." Libby clamped down any further words before throwing her briefcase on the sofa. "Fine. I'll take care of the stones. You come meet Max and Sandra Porter. They're consultants. Give them a tour of the house."

"Be happy to do so." Carl smiled broadly.

Libby picked up the box on the coffee table and checked its contents. Max gave a quizzical look. With an annoyed huff, she showed him the box. "Four stones. Rose Quartz attracts loving things. Black Tourmaline fights off negative energy. Hematite acts like a shield and citrine clears the negative and attracts the positive. I'm not a big proponent of stones, but I'm also not taking chances in this case."

"You bury these?"

"One in each corner of the property. If there's any truth to it all, the stones will help protect the house."

Max frowned. "I thought we were protecting the Darians."

Sandra slapped his shoulder hard. "I apologize for my husband. Sometimes his mouth gets the better of him. Go take care of the stones; we'll be fine in here. We'll take the tour with Carl."

Libby shot holes into Max with her glare as she walked outside.

"I'm gonna like you," Carl said. "Follow me."

He led the way through a small, modern kitchen and down a narrow staircase to a dusty basement. Wooden shelves lined the tiled floor as well as the walls. Moldy cardboard boxes filled every shelf. Old clothes and empty bottles and rusting cans filled with rustier screws crammed every available space. A new washer and dryer sat on bricks in the back with a hose running to an open drain in the floor.

Scratching his nose, Carl gestured with his elbow. "Here's the basement, if you couldn't guess. Any spookiness going on down here?"

Sandra ignored Carl as she walked up and down the two aisles. Drummond swept through the area and shook his head at Max.

"Y'know, I thought this job was going to be a bit more interesting," Carl went on. "Not that I believe in any of this, but I mean, come on. You'd think there'd be a creaking door or a thump or something."

Max blew the dust off an old album — Chubby Checker. "Why take this job if you don't believe in any of it? I can't imagine the money is any good."

"The money sucks. I could make a ton more filming weddings and birthdays. But then I'd be stuck filming weddings and birthdays."

They went back upstairs through the kitchen and living room and up to the second floor. All the while, Carl drolled on about the doldrums of filming things people wanted to pay him for. "I mean, why should I spend my days filming corporate training crap just to make a few bucks?"

"You're more of an artist."

"Nah. I don't do all that fru-fru stuff."

The second floor consisted of a straight hallway with three doors — one bathroom and two bedrooms.

Max paused at the top to let Sandra and Drummond poke about. To Carl, he said, "Then what is it you want?"

"Me? TV deal, man. That's where it's at. If this gig can land me a deal on some ghost-chasing reality show, I can use that to leverage my way into a real gig — *The Bachelor* or *The Real Housewives* or best of all, *Survivor*."

"Reality TV. I would never have guessed."

"Oh, yeah, that's the life. Get paid to film crazy people doing crazy things all over the world. No script to worry about, no shots to spend all day setting up. Just point the camera and get paid."

"I guess that would be cool." Max doubted any of it would be so easy. From what he knew, all that make-believe reality required a tremendous amount of work.

Before Carl could start talking again, Max walked down the carpeted hall. He found Sandra in the smaller of the two bedrooms. It had been decorated as a nursery with an animal-themed crib and animal-themed wallpaper. A glider/rocker, changing table, dresser, and little bookshelf completed the room.

Sandra held a stuffed elephant. She looked odd as Max entered.

"What's wrong?" he asked.

"I haven't seen anything. Not a single ghost."

Drummond floated in. "Me neither. This place is empty."

Max glanced back toward the stairs and Carl. "We heard that recording. You think they would've faked that?"

"I think people have always liked to play this game." Drummond peeked in the crib and thrust his head through the closet door. "Even in my time, there were always charlatans trying to convince anyone willing to pay up that they could talk with the dead and see the spirits and such."

"Hey, what about us?"

"Obviously, there are some people who are the real deal. All I'm saying is that people like you and Sandra are the exceptions. I don't know what's happened here to get the Darians all frazzled, but this place is empty."

"You're thinking this is a hoax, then? Libby and Jack and Carl are just trying to get on television?"

"That's my guess."

Sandra carefully placed the stuffed elephant back in the crib. "Then why did the Magi group send them to us? You think Mother Hope gives a crap about charlatans?"

Drummond leaned closer to his pocket and listened with care. "There ain't anything here," he said to his pocket. "What good would that do?" He dug into his pocket, and when he pulled back out, he cupped his hand as if carrying something delicate. "Okay, okay."

Though Max couldn't see Leed, he imagined the little globule of soul as a glowing drop of light in Drummond's palm.

"What's he want?" Sandra asked — she could see Leed, just as she saw all the dead, but only Drummond could hear the soul.

Drummond narrowed his eyes on the wall with the closet door. "He wants me to put him against the wall. Says he can sense something there."

"Well, you and I can't see anything. Might as well let the little guy give it a try."

Drummond inched toward the wall as if he expected the wood to burst out into flames. When he finally placed Leed up close, a burst arrived but not flames. Drummond and Sandra both grasped their ears and fell to the floor. Sandra cried out, her eyes shut like vices, and she curled into a ball. Drummond bellowed, his eyes bulged out, and his chest spasmed.

Max turned in a circle, searching for the cause. Though clearly his wife and partner suffered, he did not hear a thing. With no other way to help, he wrapped his arms around his wife and held her tight. Even as he whispered to her that he loved her, he wished for something more meaningful to do. From the hall, he heard footsteps stomping, and in rushed Libby and Jack.

The second they crossed the threshold, Sandra and Drummond stopped yelling. Sandra looked up at Max and lowered her hands. Breathing hard while tears dried on her cheeks, she hugged Max.

"What happened?" Libby asked while Jack pointed some type of sensor wand around the room.

Drummond thrust Leed back in his pocket. "I'll tell you what happened — this house attacked us."

As Sandra regained her composure, Max looked around the room again. He still saw nothing out of place — except, no Carl. When did that guy leave?

"Anything?" Libby asked Jack.

"I don't know what to make of this. No sounds or anything but there's an electrical pulse in the air. The kind of thing I'd expect if this was an office filled with computers and phones and all kinds of electronics."

"Get it all in the records."

Max shot to his feet. "The records? My wife was attacked by this house and you're worried about the records?"

"Honey, it's okay," Sandra said, getting to her feet with his help.

"No, it's not. You said there were no ghosts in this house. You saw nothing, yet somehow you get attacked by some super-sound. That doesn't make any sense. That sounds like a trick to me."

Libby reared back. "A trick? Are you accusing us —"

"Fraud? You bet. I don't know how you did it, but I find it interesting that the moment we get here you go off to plant magic rocks while Jack, the sound guy, disappears from sight and Carl takes the long way round so that we don't end up in this room until last. Then we're left alone and having seen not a single speck or sign of ghosts, suddenly my wife and my partner are attacked by some special frequency audio thing. This reeks of a set up."

"I will not have my integrity slandered." Libby's eyes burned as she snapped her fingers in Max's face. "Get the hell out of this house."

"Gladly."

Libby stood at the top of the staircase. "I better never see you again at any house. You don't come into my work and call me a fraud. I'll see that nobody wants to hire you."

Max escorted Sandra back to the car. She resisted a bit, but the attack had left her too weak to argue. Drummond floated in the back seat before Max had turned the engine over.

As they drove away, he could still hear Libby shouting.

Chapter 5

MAX TURNED ONTO SILAS CREEK PARKWAY and wound his way around the city toward Wake Forest University. They had bought a beautiful home in the wealthier neighborhoods nearby, and Max wanted to get Sandra into bed for some rest. Both she and Drummond had their heads arched back and their eyes closed. Sweat beaded on her brow.

After only a few minutes, Sandra's attention perked up. "Where are you going?"

"Home. You can take it easy for the rest of the day."

She groaned as she shook her head. "Turn around. Go back to the office."

"Why? We're off the case."

"Like hell we are."

Sandra's harsh tone snapped against Drummond. He popped forward and said, "I've got no intention of listening to you two bicker. It's worse than getting a lecture from an old schoolmarm. I'll be at my bookshelf, if you need me."

Before Max could utter a response, Drummond dissipated.

"I mean it," Sandra went on. "Turn around. We are not dropping this case."

Max pulled into the Parkway Presbyterian Church lot and stopped the car. He flexed his fingers against the steering wheel. "I didn't want to take this case from the beginning, and I'm pretty sure Drummond didn't want it, either. You accepted it before we even had a chance to talk as a group."

"I'm sorry about that. But we did accept the case, and we can't back away simply because it became difficult."

"That's not it at all. I don't trust this Libby Broward and her friends. The whole thing stinks."

"That attack was not a hoax. Something is in that house."

"I believe you, but that doesn't mean Broward is legit. Besides, don't you think haunted houses are a bit pedestrian for us?"

"You think we should sit around and wait for the next Hull calamity to strike?"

"That's not what I mean."

"It's exactly what you mean. It really bothers you that Cecily Hull is out there plotting the takeover of her family and the demise of Tucker Hull, and you're not a part of it." Max tried to protest, but Sandra shut him down by raising her index finger. "You've been fighting them for several years now. It's hard to let that go. But Cecily doesn't trust us any more than we trust her. She paid us for our work and thankfully, we haven't heard from her since. As long as the Hulls are fighting each other, we should be thrilled to stay out of it."

Max peered outside. "I know. I really do. And I have no death wish. I'm not waiting around hoping for the Hulls to need us. But there is a weird thing about them — a draw to the danger, maybe."

"Forget about them. We have a chance right now to help a couple of decent people survive the dangers they're living inside of daily — danger that isn't the result of some nasty plan gone awry or anything else a Hull might have conceived. We can help the little guy."

Max grew silent. Cars zipped along the parkway and he remained still. Maybe Sandra was right. Maybe, if he could be honest about it, maybe the danger of dealing with the Hulls brought with it so much adrenaline, so much suspense, so much excitement, that he had become addicted to it.

Sandra rubbed the side of her head. "Be careful, honey. You're changing."

"What are you talking about? How?"

"I mean, the Max Porter I fell in love with would never hesitate to take the side of the little guy. Anything to thumb his nose at the one percent."

"Getting older and having responsibilities changed both of us."

"Not like this. I think it's the money that got you."

"What money? You mean what we earned from Cecily?"

Sandra nodded. "We've never had so much in our life. Look at us. New house, new office, new car. But I can see your wheels turning every time we spend anything. You're not worried about helping the little guy anymore. You're starting to worry about holding on to all that money."

"You want to be poor again? Go back to living in a trailer?"

"I don't want to sell out ourselves for a flatscreen and good air conditioning." She leaned over and kissed his cheek. "Besides, doesn't it make more sense to make a little money now, instead of waiting around for a big case that might never come?"

Max's hand touched the keys but then pulled back. "What's this really about? You've been strange lately. Withdrawn. Then suddenly you want this case, and now you want it so bad, you're not even worried that we're being conned. Something's going on with you."

"It's nothing. No need to be concerned."

"I'm your husband. I love you. Of course, I'm going to be concerned."

"Look at it this way — if Libby Broward is pulling off a hoax, then the Darians don't know it. You saw the fear when they visited us. That wasn't fake. Shouldn't we debunk Broward to protect the Darians from being exploited? But if this is not a hoax, the Darians are in serious danger and Broward has already admitted she can't handle it alone. The Darians need us. Either way, hoax or not, we've got to stay on the case for them."

Max turned the ignition, the keys rattling an unmistakable anger. Despite his frustrations, he drove back to the city and their office. He could feel Sandra suppressing a victorious smile. No — she never would gloat other than as a jest. Yet he had a wriggling sense of it that he couldn't pinpoint down like a shifting movement in his peripheral vision — there but not there.

By the time they reached the office, he had looped and wound and twisted his thoughts into a spaghetti of suspicions — none of which added up to anything useful. Their tactic when faced with such a confusing situation had often consisted of shoving their way forward. But he didn't know what path could be called forward — work for Broward, work against Broward, help the Darians at all costs, question if the Darians are in on it, if there was an *it* to be in on.

When they entered the office, Drummond swept out of the bookshelf with a cautious but expectant enthusiasm. "You two kids work everything out?"

"Of course, we did," Sandra said. "We're all still working on the Darian case. But we're keeping our eyes open for any irregularities, anything that might suggest Libby Broward is running a con on these people."

"You got it. What's our plan?"

Max slumped behind his desk. "Nothing for you, right now, unless you want to help with doing the research."

"Think I'll pass on that one."

Sandra brought her hand to her cheek with a ridiculously overacted move. "Oh, dear, I completely forgot. I'm sorry, hon, but you'll have to start the research alone. I've got an appointment."

"For what?"

"Just an appointment. I'll be back in a few hours."

Max watched her pull together her things, grab her keys, and walk out. He faced Drummond. "I'm not crazy, right? She's acting strange."

Drummond crossed his arms. "She's definitely not being herself."

"You don't think —"

"What?"

"Nothing."

Drummond scowled. "Don't you dare start thinking ill thoughts of that gal. She's the most loyal person I've ever met."

"I know, I know. It's just ... well, things at home have been rather cold lately."

"What in the world makes you think I want to know about that?"

"Because we're worried about her and I think you should know that her behavior has been different at home, too. And frankly, it's been my experience that when things start slagging off in the bedroom, it's a sure sign that you got problems elsewhere."

"Yeah? It's been my experience that a husband shouldn't be talking about his wife's bedroom habits with anybody but his wife."

Max smacked his desk causing the pens to rattle. "Stop being a prude and pay attention. I'm telling you things aren't right with her. I'm not saying she's cheating on me. Lord knows that better not be it. But something is off. So, do me a favor, please. Go follow her. Find out what this secret appointment is all about."

Drummond acted as if warding off an attack. "That's a really bad idea. Remember, I spent many years as a PI before I was murdered. I've been hired by countless jealous husbands, and I'm telling you for a fact, no good will come to your marriage by following her."

"But I'm worried —"

"So am I. Following her like a criminal is not the answer. If she's doing something she shouldn't, you probably don't really want to know. And if it's all innocent, then you'll feel guilty for doubting her. Regardless of the answer, if she catches on, you're screwed. In all the times I've done work of this kind, I promise you, not once did it end well — no matter what the truth was."

Max shook his head like a teacher losing his patience. "I've heard you. Now, please, go find out what she's doing. Don't get seen. As long as it's nothing that threatens my marriage or her life, as long as you think it's best I don't know, then come back and tell me it's all fine. I promise I won't push it any further. I won't have to know anything more. Is that okay? Does that jive with your marriage counseling?"

"Jive?"

"You know what I mean."

Drummond mulled over the idea before tipping his hat. "You got it. I'll report in as soon as I can."

Once the ghost had left, Max released a long sigh. Not even two o'clock on the first day of the case, and the whole world had flipped on him. He should never have left his bed that morning.

At least, for the rest of the day, he could submerge in the depths of research. Life always felt better between the pages of books. Certainly safer than chasing ghosts. Though, research often meant the same thing — but the ghosts in history didn't attack him from the books. Not yet, anyway.

Max opened his laptop but did not turn it on. He had no desire to stare at a computer screen for the next few hours. He needed to clear his head, to get lost in tactile research, to put aside all these things he could not control.

Snatching his keys, he donned his coat and stopped at Sandra's desk. He jotted a quick note: *Gone to the library.* As he left the office, he discovered a lightness in his step. The library awaited him, and that would be the best way to turn his day around.

He hoped.

Chapter 6

THE Z. SMITH REYNOLDS LIBRARY at Wake Forest University consisted of two old buildings with the wide alley between converted into a study area complete with desks, chairs, computers, and an atrium ceiling that washed the students in sunlight. Max loved it. Even more than the beautiful repurposing of the buildings, Max enjoyed the numerous hidden nooks.

He found one such hideaway on the third floor. Not so much hidden as simply seldom used. He settled in with his laptop and a few volumes by local authors.

But he came up empty.

At least, empty of anything big. He did learn that the house dated back to the early 1920s, and for a short time, he thought he had a significant lead. The ghost music Jack had recorded had sounded like something from that era. Maybe a band had been slaughtered in the attic.

Except it ended there. Max searched the newspapers and databases, but nothing came up for that address. The house had endured an uneventful existence.

His researching instincts took over, and he turned his focus on North Carolina as a whole in the 1920s. This turned up a few interesting dates — particularly around the subject of Prohibition. In 1919, the United States passed the 18th Amendment outlawing alcohol and the law went into use at the start of 1920. By that time, however, North Carolina had been a dry state for almost twenty years.

In the early 1900s, North Carolina had been consumed by the problems of alcoholism, much of it blamed on the Civil

War. Those that had fought were in their sixties, and many suffered from PTSD without any mental professionals in existence to help. The majority of those men self-medicated and did so quite hard. Incidents of public drunkenness and spousal abuse related to alcohol rose sharply.

In response, the temperance movement gained steam. They protested the behavior and saw alcohol as the evil that caused it all. It took several years, but with the help of Governor Thomas Jarvis in 1906, North Carolina became an official dry state. Unofficially, of course, the booze continued to flow, and if the country had been paying attention, they would have seen that going dry would only lead to organized crime.

While Max found all of this fascinating, he had to admit that none of it helped in regards to the case. No murders, no tragedies, no kind of unexplained horrors could be linked to the Darians' house. He rubbed his eyes and closed the book on Prohibition he had been reading.

"Getting anywhere?" a voice asked.

Max clenched his teeth. He knew the voice — Leon Moore. "What do you want?"

The old, black librarian offered a placating smile as he approached. Tall and bald, he walked with a limp and a slight bend to his back, but that didn't fool Max. Old Leon worked with Mother Hope — leader of the Magi group — and that gave him access to serious magic.

Leon put out his hand. "I wanted to thank you for helping my friends."

"Don't. I'm only doing this because Sandra said we would. The second I found out it was all connected to your little Magi group, I wanted nothing to do with it."

"The Magi group isn't connected. I know Wayne Darian through librarian circles. I happened to overhear him discussing his problems, and I offered to assist. That's all. Honestly."

"Your track record with honesty isn't too good."

Leon's face wrinkled as his brow tightened. "Here's a little honesty for you. You are one of the most difficult people I've ever met."

"Coming from you, that's a compliment."

"I'm sorry you feel that way. I only wanted to thank you and offer whatever help I can give, but you clearly don't want it. I'll leave you be." He turned away, paused, and whirled back. "I don't understand you. The Magi group exists to fight the Hulls, the very people who have spun your life in a tornado ever since you stepped foot in North Carolina. Why would you think we're the enemy?"

Max leaned his chair back. "Maybe it has something to do with the fact that you watched the Hulls do all that to me and my wife and never helped us until you had no choice. Yeah, you think that might be it?"

"You stupid fool. Do you really believe we did nothing all that time? Just because you don't know about something, doesn't mean it didn't happen. You're worse than a fool. You think you fought the Hulls and won all on your own — not once, but over and over."

"So now you're claiming to have saved my ass all along? Yet your sweet leader has gone out of her way to threaten me to stay away."

"For your own safety. You know the history of that family better than anyone. And you tell me — in all their centuries of existence, has there ever been anybody who has a record like yours against them?"

Max paused. Leon had a point. If anybody managed to best the Hulls more than once, they usually ended up disappearing. "Perhaps you've been an aid once or twice. But we never asked for your help, and I feel no obligation towards you."

"Nor would I ever expect such a thing from you. Which is why I came over here to thank you for helping the Darians instead of demanding your help."

"Fine. You're welcome. Please leave."

Disgusted, Leon shuffled off. A moment later, however, he returned. "I'm trying to understand something about you. Why do you do this? Whether you like us or not, the Magi group exists to help protect the world from people like the Hulls. That's the good side of magic — helping people. But you act like it's a burden to help others. Why do you do it then, if not to help?"

Max pushed the book on Prohibition towards Leon. "Those people were just trying to help. That didn't turn out so good. As for me and Sandra — we've been trying to survive. That's all. Fighting the Hulls, helping those we've helped — none of that was for any other reason than survival. But now we have enough money that we don't worry if there'll be food on the table. So, we don't have to take every case that comes to us. We don't have to fight every battle that falls before us. Understand? We've fought it out already. We won. Can't you people let us breathe in peace for a little?"

"I see," Leon said, and Max swore the man had aged since his arrival. "Let me say this before I leave you to your peace. Please do not bring any of this case to the Magi group. They truly do not know about it, and I do not wish to burden Mother Hope with more than she already must deal with. It would only aid our mutual enemies."

"Why would I ever bring anything to her? The only hope I have concerning her is that I hope never to see her again."

"Then I guess that's it. Goodbye."

The old man limped away, leaving this final plea hanging in the air. Max doubted Leon cared about Mother Hope's burden. Rather it seemed more likely that Leon was working outside the confines of the Magi group. But the idea that Leon had gone rogue didn't ring true. Maybe, quite simply, he really did want to help this family.

And what does it say about me that I keep trying to get out of it? That thought sent uncomfortable chills through Max.

His entire argument about not really wanting to help people but merely survive rang more false than anything Leon had said. Sandra would have called him out on it right away. Helping people had been the whole point — maybe not with their first case, but certainly ever since facing the Hulls. They didn't want anybody to suffer because of such powerful families or because of ghosts or curses or any of the things they had come into personal contact with. That was the truth, but

Max tried to shake it off. Protecting Sandra had to come first.

Drummond appeared through the ceiling. Max barely moved — *I've gotten far too comfortable with that.* However, he wasn't comfortable with Drummond's expression.

"What's wrong?"

"Hurry," Drummond said, circling his hand to get Max packing up. "Your wife's in trouble."

Chapter 7

AS THEY DROVE, Max peppered Drummond with questions, but the ghost refused to answer. He kept his eyes forward and his jaw held tight. When Max launched another barrage of questions, Drummond pushed back his hat with an exasperated huff.

"Look," Drummond said, "I'm not trying to be mysterious or coy or anything. You'll see when we get there. I don't know what it all means, and if I tell you what I saw, you'll just ask me more things I don't know the answer to. But I do know enough to say that it ain't good and that if we don't do something about it, she'll be in serious trouble sooner or later."

"Was that supposed to ease my mind?"

"That was supposed to get you to shut up."

Max snapped his mouth closed. He pulled onto Knollwood Street and turned into a large strip mall. On the near end, the ground dropped low enough to create a bottom floor for a few stores. A Hanes outlet provided a cheap dumping ground for Hanes products that couldn't sell elsewhere. Next door was where they would find Sandra. The restaurant was now called Ham's — a sports bar with bright red, yellow, and black trim. The place had televisions mounted everywhere, including one mounted on the wall to entertain those dining outside. But Max knew it under its former name — the Fox & Hound.

"See?" Drummond said as they got out of the car. "Things have changed here. I followed Sandra straight from the office, and she took one look at the new ownership and her whole demeanor changed."

No. Max knew it had nothing to do with the ownership.

Drummond knew it too, but the old ghost hadn't been there that night. He knew what had happened, but he didn't go through it.

Drummond nodded toward the back of the building. "After a while, she kind of stumbled that way toward the alley. That's where she should be now, not in the restaurant but in the alley."

Max nodded. That's where it had all happened — a year ago, the ghost of Patricia Welling, a witch who once loved Drummond, had possessed Sandra and attempted to seduce Max. When he saw through the ruse, she cried out for help and a bunch of young college boys, thinking they were saving the lady, beat Max to a pulp.

Drummond pulled up his coat collar as if it were a cold, rainy night instead of a warm dusk. "I don't like to admit this, but sometimes the fairer sex is a bit of a mystery to me. I suspect that's true of all men. I mean, do you really understand all the things your wife does?"

Max stopped under a red awning with HAM'S written across the top. "No. I don't think I do."

"That's my point."

"But I keep trying." A sly grin lifted on his lips. "That's one of those things that separate the men from the boys."

Max turned the corner to find Sandra standing in the alley near the dumpsters. She stared at the brick wall where her possessed-self had moved on him not so long ago. She rubbed her arms as if fighting off a chill while her focus never wavered.

Perhaps she relived the incident. Max didn't know all the symptoms of PTSD, but it made sense that she might be suffering. Except she never seemed to have a problem with all the things they had been through before, and they had endured a few more traumatic cases since Patricia Welling and the witch coven. Could PTSD delay in a person until something triggered it off? She certainly had been behaving strangely in the last few weeks.

"I couldn't do anything," she said, her voice breaking the quiet like shattering glass. "I was inside my head and I saw what was happening out here, but I couldn't do anything to stop it."

Max approached her and gently laid a hand on her shoulder. "You didn't have to. I saw through her disguise. I knew she wasn't you."

"Not at first. Not until the last moment, really. In fact, if you hadn't caught on when you did, you would have had sex with her thinking it was me."

"But that didn't happen."

Sandra stepped away from Max's hand. "Ever since that case, I've thought about this moment, about what could have happened. It wouldn't have bothered me — the sex, I mean. If it had happened, you would have been thinking you were with me. It's not like you would have been knowingly cheating on me or anything."

"It still would have felt like cheating. Heck, I feel bad about kissing her or you or however you want to think about it. I can see why it spins your head a bit. But why dwell on it? I did figure it out before anything bad happened. It all turned out okay."

Her fingers traced the bricks where her possessed body had braced herself that night, ready for Max to take her. "What would have happened if you had done it here that night? What if I had become pregnant?"

"Sheesh, honey, why would you want to think such a dark thing?"

She whirled back on him, her eyes blazing. "Because it almost happened. Even if it didn't this time, that doesn't mean it can't or won't ever happen. And if we could come so close to that kind of a twisted tragedy, then what about those who aren't in touch with the truth of the supernatural? What of people like Shawnee Darian? What might those forces be doing to her unborn child?"

"Ah," Max said, all the dots lining up. "I think I see. This case isn't about Libby or the house or any of that. It's really about Shawnee Darian and her baby."

"I thought I've been quite clear on that point."

"You probably have. I don't think I could see quite beyond

Libby. I'm sorry."

Sandra wrapped her arms around Max's waist and rested her head on his chest. "I'm not the one you really need to apologize to."

Max winced. "Do I really have to?"

"Do you really need to ask?"

"Okay, okay. I'll make nice with Libby."

"Good, because I called her earlier and set up a meeting tonight in the Darian house. She said we'd have a better chance of spotting activity at night."

"I swear this has been the longest day ever. Coffee and bagels feels like it was a year ago."

Sandra leaned back and looked down the alley. "Drummond? You can come out now."

Drummond sauntered around the corner and approached as if nothing unusual had occurred. "Y'all having a good time back here?"

"The best. I should get possessed more often."

Max forced a smile though none of them liked the joke. "We're going back to the Darian house for the night. See what happens."

Drummond hesitated. "Did you get hit in the head? You forget what happened to Sandra and me? That hurt."

"Don't worry," Sandra said. "You're not coming along. I think your time would be better spent searching the Other for any ghosts that were associated with the house. Surely somebody out there knows what happened here."

"You got it. I'll find something." To Max, he added, "You watch out for her. That house ain't right. It's another lesson you both need to keep learning — just because we've survived some pretty tough spots, doesn't make us invincible. You've got to be careful."

As Drummond left, Max and Sandra walked back to the car. Max agreed with the warning — especially for Sandra. She had become so focused on Shawnee and the baby that she didn't appear to take seriously the dangers of what she had experienced. Or maybe that was his own fears talking. Either way, he figured it would be better to stand by her side and back her up than be outside the house, unable to help her should the need arise.

Still, one thing bothered him. "Why did you hide all this stuff from me? You could have opened up to me about it."

"I wasn't hiding anything. I was waiting. I was dealing with it until I could tell you. When it all started, I couldn't really explain what I was feeling, and I knew if I had said anything, you'd bombard me with questions that I couldn't answer. So, I waited."

"I see," Max said, and though her explanation made sense, a shiver in her voice suggested that she still hid the full story.

"Being here, I thought, would help me articulate it all, get it clear in my head. And it did. Had you not shown up when you did, I would've gone back to the office and told you everything. How did you find me here, anyway?"

Max got in the car. "I was just coming to grab a bite when Drummond noticed you."

"At Ham's?"

"Thought I'd give it a try. Not really hungry anymore, though." Max thought about glass houses and stones. "Besides, I've got some apologizing to do."

They drove off to the Darian house, both remaining quiet and uncomfortable the entire ride.

Chapter 8

UPON ENTERING THE DARIAN HOME, Sandra hugged Libby like they were old friends. Max fidgeted in the doorway, keenly aware of the unwelcoming eyes upon him. Carl glared from the back corner as he wired a new camera while Jack plunked down the stairs and bumped Max's shoulder on his way to the kitchen.

"Ms. Broward," Max said, clearing his throat, "do you have a minute?"

Libby walked straight towards him. "We have a lot of important work to do tonight, and I really don't want to fight. Thank you for bringing your wife by. I promise we'll take good care of her."

"There's been some confusion. I'm not leaving her here."

"But I thought she was going to help us."

"She is, and I will, too. Look, I know I can get loud and vocal and all that when I feel passionate about something. It doesn't mean I'm angry."

Libby stepped out of Carl's way as he strung cables into the kitchen. "You shouted at me and called me a fraud. Let's not pretend you weren't angry."

"That's not what I'm trying to say. I simply mean that I can overreact at times."

Libby waited, but when Max said no more, she shook her head like a disappointed teacher. "That's it? You came out here to tell me that you overreact? I already knew that. I saw it firsthand."

"I'm trying to apologize."

"Maybe you should have started with actually apologizing."

Max held a breath before letting it out slow. "I'm sorry. I truly am. Something about this case has really set me off-balance, and I took it out on you. But we're supposed to be here to help the Darians, and that's what Sandra and I want to do."

"Okay. I suppose that's the best I can expect to get from you. Let's get to work." Libby turned to the kitchen and raised one finger, ticking off her point. "I want to be clear — I don't have the time or the patience to have all my decisions called into question. You are here to help our investigation. We are not here to serve you. Understand?"

"You got it."

"Then welcome to GWC — Ghost Watching Central."

The kitchen had been transformed into an electronic ghost surveillance room. Four monitors spied on all the rooms and halls in the house. Each monitor held a view for several seconds before switching to another camera. A fifth monitor displayed in infrared. Three laptops ran numerous programs — some audio, some visual, some Max couldn't be sure about. Thick cables snaked from the setup into the rest of the house.

Jack crossed his feet on the table in the only clear spot available. On his lap rested a wireless keyboard that appeared to control everything. He sipped a mug of coffee and nodded at Max.

"Help yourself," Jack said, indicating the three coffee makers on the kitchen counter.

Max grabbed a mug from a hanging rack under the cabinets. "You guys really like coffee."

"Only way I'm going to make it through the night, man. Whatever is happening in this house usually likes making itself known after about one in the morning."

Libby slid out a chair and sat next to Jack. Behind her, on the floor, Max noticed a pile of pillows and blankets. "Might as well settle in," she said. "We'll try to make contact throughout the night, but so far, there's been no response until after one. That's when Jack recorded the music you heard."

Sandra said, "You don't call what happened to me this

afternoon a response?"

"I don't know what that was. But that's one reason we'll try throughout the night. It seems you may be able to draw it out earlier. Whatever *it* is."

Max offered a mug to Sandra but she waved it off. She looked uncomfortable — not that Max thought anything at the moment should feel comfortable. "You okay?"

Sandra trembled out a smile. "Just anxious, I guess." To Libby, she said, "I want to see the baby's room, again."

Max gestured toward the monitors. "You'll be able to watch everything that happens to us up there, right?"

"That's the idea," Jack said.

Sandra placed a hand on Max's arm, and he knew what she would say. He closed his eyes, hoping he'd be wrong.

"Hon," she said, and her tone confirmed his fears. "I don't want you up there. Libby will come with me." Before he could utter a protest, she went on, "You can watch me from in here, but I need to focus while I'm in that room. I need to be on my guard in case that attack happens again, and it'll be harder for me with you there. Part of me will be concerned about you, about your safety. I can't have my mind split on two different concerns while I'm in that space."

With his lips locked tight, Max backed against the counter to allow Libby enough room to pass. Sandra pecked his cheek and the two women left the room. Max plopped in Libby's chair and set his coffee mug on the table with a loud thunk.

When the women started on the stairs, Jack said, "Dude, that was cold."

"She didn't mean it in a bad way."

"Oh, I know, but still."

Max held back his comments. What this man thought of Sandra and their relationship meant nothing. He finally settled on, "I understand her. It's fine."

Jack leaned over the arm of his chair, peeking around the doorway. He zipped back to Max and reached into his coat pocket. Offering a pitiful grin as he pulled out a hip flask, he said in a conspiratorial whisper, "If we've got to be stuck down here all night, might as well have a little fun. Am I right?" He tipped the flasks contents into his coffee before holding it above Max's mug.

Max placed a hand over the steaming coffee. "No, thanks."

"Sure?"

"I need the coffee to keep awake all night. Booze is only going to make that harder. By the smell of that, it would probably knock me out."

Jack chuckled. "It is strong."

On the grainy monitors, Max watched as Sandra and Libby approached the baby's room. They paused at the door before entering. Once inside, they spoke softly for a moment before sitting in the center of the floor.

Clacking on the keyboard, Jack turned up the volume on the monitors. He then adjusted the mix on the microphones recording in the baby's room.

Libby shrugged and in full voice said, "Will the spirit inside this house please make itself known?"

All remained silent.

"Spirit of this house, we want to speak with you. We are here to help."

Nothing.

Libby and Sandra leaned back against the crib and waited. Jack sipped from his spiked mug. "See that? It's going to be a very long night."

Max nodded. "It's entirely possible nothing will happen, right?"

"Oh, sure. Plenty of times — heck most of the times — nothing ever happens. But when it does, oh, man does it ever happen. I've seen some crazy, crazy shit. Stuff moving by itself. Flickering lights and closing doors where there ain't anybody around."

"Sounds frightening."

Jack pointed at Max. "Oh, I must sound like an idiot. I mean I only really ever hear them and see stuff on the monitors. Most of the time what I get to hear ain't all that clear. But you actually see them, don't you?"

"Just one."

"Is he in here?"

"No. We're alone."

Jack sipped more of his coffee as his eyes roved about the kitchen. "That's real creepy."

"Why would that be creepy to you? Don't you do this all the time?"

"Yeah, but it's different knowing you can see one, see it all pale and stuck in the time it died."

Max looked away from the monitor. "How do you know what they look like?"

Jack paused, then chuckled with a guilty smile. "I must've drunk a little too fast. I wanted to say that ghosts are supposed to look like that, but I couldn't get it out. Truth is I've seen one once. Not on a case. Long time ago. That's what got me doing this."

As Jack continued talking, Max focused back on the monitor. He watched Sandra's image, trying to will away anything evil.

"See, it was back when I was in college," Jack said. "I had some friends who lived in this old, renovated house, and on Halloween they'd throw this wicked party. Do the whole place up in skeletons and stuff. Real big blast."

Max thought about the things Sandra had said in the alley. It had been hanging between them for years now, and he hadn't even known. Except this wasn't like the secrets they had kept from each other in the past. They had learned from those mistakes. They had done well at keeping things honest.

"So, one time at this Halloween party — I think it was my junior year — I got really plastered. I mean I'd never been that drunk before and certainly never since. I remember this cute girl just fell into my lap and we laughed and talked and she invited me back to her place. I remember she went to get her coat. And you know what happened after that?" Jack snorted. "I ain't got a clue."

Max tried to understand Sandra's view. The remnants of being possessed by a dead witch clung to her. They were strands of marionette string hung into the air but held by nobody. They left Sandra in a weird predicament — feeling like she wasn't completely her own.

"When I finally woke up, I was in the attic of that house. It was so dark. I had reached that stage where everything spun, and I totally blew chunks. Felt a little better, so I tried sitting up. And that's when I saw her. This pale figure floating a good foot in the air. She wore this ratty dress, looked like something from the 1800s. And she stared at me. Freaked me out. I ran downstairs and out of that house screaming. I can still hear my friends laughing. So, I thought the whole thing was a joke."

This case, this chance to help Shawnee, must have hit Sandra hard. Max could see it now. This case was about coping with trauma.

"But my buddy denied any kind of set up. Next night, I went and did a bunch of research, and I found her. Died in 1872 when an oil lamp hung on the attic beam fell on her head. Lit her up fast, but with all those layers of clothes they wore back then, it took her a while to die. Well, after that I started hanging with the paranormal people and that led a long, winding road to me sitting right here with you."

Max thought back over Sandra's recent behavior. Sleepless nights, strange mood swings, and her odd, undefined excursions — all added up to her struggling to make sense of what had happened. *And I have to be here for her.* That was one of many changes Max had tried to make of late. He didn't have to fix her problems, but he did have to be there for her when she needed him. Even if that meant nothing more than sitting in the kitchen watching her on the monitors.

"Dude," Jack said, refilling Max's mug with coffee. "You better drink up if you're going to be that intense. I'm not kidding when I say these nights can go real long."

* * * *

DAY TWO

The hours drifted by. Despite the coffee, both Max and Jack nodded off a few times. Never for long, but guilt coursed through Max each time.

While awake, he glued himself to the monitors. Libby paced the baby's room, then stared out the window, then checked out the crib, then poked around the closet, then sat, then stood, then started all over again. Sandra hardly moved. Max had never known her to meditate, but she appeared to be an expert at it — sitting still, eyes closed, breathing deep, hyper-aware yet calm.

Jack passed gas as he typed on his keyboard. "Excuse me," he muttered.

The noise snapped Max's attention off of Sandra. "Didn't know you were awake."

"When I'm on the job, I'm always awake. Even when I'm asleep, I'm awake."

Max glanced at the clock — 2:32 a.m. "Is there a cut-off point? A time when you guys call it quits for the night?"

"Yup. It's called sunrise."

As his eyes roved across all the monitors, Max froze. "Where's Carl?"

"I don't know. I think he went out to find some hot food. Not much of anything open at this hour. Just a few diners, but he always manages to come back with something good for everybody."

"In that case, I hope he brings —"

Whomp!

The sudden blow to the house came from all sides. One solid hit that shook the walls and floors and rattled the windows. It carried a dark sound like tombstones falling on a wooden platform.

Jack shot forward, his fingers furious on the keyboard. Max watched the monitors. He saw Sandra and Libby standing in the baby's room, their heads slowly moving as they scanned the room.

"I can't hear anything from there," Max said.

"Hold on." Jack flipped switches and typed more on the keyboard. "Whatever that was popped a few mics. It's not like they're the highest end, y'know."

Max jumped to his feet, leaning closer to the monitor. "We've got to be able to hear in there. We've got to know what's going on."

"Relax. There's a reason I'm good at what I do." He tapped two more keys and the sound ignited around them. "I always put in backups."

Libby had her hands clutched against her chest. After a few moments passed without the noise returning, she gave a thumbs-up sign to the camera.

Max looked to Jack. "What's that about? What's so good?"

"She's feeling a presence. She's going to try to make contact."

Sandra stood firm next to Libby, but Max caught the tremors in her hands. "I should go up there," he said. "My wife is —"

"You should stay here. You go in there and you'll interrupt whatever is going on. Breaking in on an established moment like this, it's like cockroaches running when the lights are flicked on. Get me?"

Libby closed her eyes, and Max swore she was offering a prayer. Then she looked up at the ceiling and said, "Who are you?"

No answer.

"Why are you here?"

No answer.

"Can you make a noise for me?"

Jack frowned. "Huh."

"What?" Max snapped.

"Those are all standard questions — the kind of thing that any ghost hunting group would ask."

"So?"

"Not Libby's style. She prefers the methods of John Sabol — to ask questions based on the history of the house, the land, the people involved, anything that's more personal and specific to the entity. But she's starting out with the basic stuff. That's not usual."

"And? What about it?"

Jack shrugged. "If I had to guess, I'd say she was a little scared and was reverting back to the basics as a way to regain her composure."

"Wait — you're saying that the woman who is up there to protect my wife is freaking out?"

"What I'm saying is —"

Whomp! Whomp!

Max grabbed the edge of the wooden table, a splinter digging into his palm. Dust fell from the hanging ceiling lamp and two glasses toppled over in the sink.

Libby said, "We heard the music you played. The music from the twenties. Is that when you're from? Did you die in the twenties?"

The banging grew louder and continued to shake the house. On the monitor, Max watched as a lamp next to the crib shattered. Sandra leaped out of the way as Libby yelped.

Jack typed furiously, his eyes wide and lips quivering. "This is off the charts. I've never seen anything remotely close."

The shaking eased back. Max steadied his legs as he strode toward the stairs.

Looking up from his work, Jack said, "Hey, what are you doing?"

"You're nuts if you think I'm staying here while my wife is being threatened."

Max hopped up the stairs and rushed down the hall. As he burst into the baby's room, he saw Sandra kneeling on the floor while Libby raised her arms toward the ceiling.

"Please," Libby said. "We're here to listen. Tell us what you want."

The house thumped like a massive heart pulsing around them. Cracks traveled up the walls and across the ceiling. All the lights flicked on and off. The floor lurched to the right. A loud creaking filled the air like the whine of tearing metal as a boat sinks beneath the ocean.

But the house did not sink. In fact, Max caught a glimpse of two people passing on the sidewalk outside — neither appeared to take notice of the house. Could this all be some sort of illusion? A hallucination?

"We're not here to harm you," Libby shouted above the constant banging. "We offer help. We offer peace."

Max stumbled across and took hold of Sandra. She buried her face in the crook of his arm. He could feel her shivering. He had never heard the previous attack, and that one had hurt her badly. How much worse would this be since he could hear it all now?

A surge of electricity snaked from the wall outlets up to the ceiling, breaking apart drywall as it moved. The room brightened in stark light and the banging reached a fevered rhythm.

Then all went dark.

An odd clunk hit near the door.

Max kissed the back of Sandra's head. They were both covered in drywall dust and breathing hard. A new thumping — Jack coming up the stairs.

"Everyone okay?" he called.

"We're fine," Libby said. "You get all that?"

"I hope so. As far as I can tell, everything's recording perfectly. Y'all just stay still. I'll go downstairs and reset the circuit breakers."

"Thank you. And thanks for recording it all." Max could hear Libby's smile. "This may turn out to be the greatest documented case ever."

A few minutes went by, and soon the hall lights clicked back on. Sitting in the doorway, Max saw a blue bottle. As Libby moved closer towards it, Max straightened. A second later, Sandra stood by his side.

Libby lifted the bottle — about the size of a wine bottle and clear blue all around. "Is this what made that last sound?"

Max put out his hand. “May I?”

She held out the bottle but was slow to let go. Max examined it. “Looks like your ghost has a sense of humor.”

“Oh?”

He pointed to the name printed into the blue glass — CASPER.

Chapter 9

THE MORNING SUN STILL HAD TO WAIT a few hours as Max pulled into the driveway of their new home. Neither he nor Sandra had ever owned a newly constructed home before — one that no other person had ever slept in, ate in, lived in. The all-brick house stood on a third of an acre like a castle nestled amongst numerous other castles in a neighborhood where all the street names were related to Robin Hood (Sherwood Drive, Nottingham Road, and the most obvious, Robin Hood Road). Clicking the remote to open the garage, Max took a moment to marvel at the idea that this all belonged to him.

His bones crackled as he climbed out of the car. He cradled the blue bottle marked CASPER like a delicate newborn. Libby had put up a fuss when he took it, and only backed off when Sandra promised they would return it while also emphasizing Max's excellent researching skills. Libby acquiesced but not without scowling and grumbling.

Sandra had slept the entire drive home and now stirred from her slumber like a drunken co-ed paying for a long night out. Only, in Sandra's case, she didn't get to have any fun. She poured out of the passenger side and uttered a non-committal sound as she headed toward Max.

As the garage door rumbled down, he stared at the alarm keypad by the kitchen entrance. Ten seconds clicked by before he could recall the code. Sandra pressed her head against his back while she waited.

When they finally stepped inside the kitchen, Sandra mumbled a few indecipherable words and staggered upstairs to bed. Max threw his coat on the marble counter, set the blue bottle down, and threw on a pot of coffee. As tired as he felt, he knew he had gone past the point of falling asleep. Wired on adrenaline and caffeine, he figured he would focus on the case until he either discovered something important or passed out.

He grabbed the bottle, walked across the kitchen, stepped into a sunken living room, and through a door that opened into his study. *A study*. The idea that he lived in a house big enough to furnish a study still prickled his skin. The Darians had no such luxuries, despite both holding excellent jobs, and all they wanted was a place that wasn't trying to kill them or possess their baby.

"Okay, Casper, time to find out about you."

Max inspected the bottle with care. Cobalt blue with a fluted neck, the bottle had distinct ribbing that traveled from the mouth down to the shoulders. The name CASPER, curving to follow part of a circle, could be read with ease, but the rest of the engraving had been worn away.

Googling *blue casper bottle* returned instant hits. Max clicked on the images tab and saw dozens of bottles similar to the one sitting on his desk. Along with the blue bottles, the search results included several brown and tan whiskey jugs. The stamped labels on those jugs were easy to read.

FROM THE CASPER CO.
WINSTON-SALEM, NC
LOWEST PRICE WHISKEY HOUSE
SEND FOR CONFIDENTIAL PRICE LIST

From there, the searching went even easier. In no time, Max waded through article after article detailing the life of the Casper family and their involvement in the whiskey trade.

It all began in 1861 when the grandfather of John L. Casper set up a couple of stills in North Carolina. They were used for the family — mostly — and served to keep everyone happy through hard times. John L.'s father, John C. Casper, joined the unofficial company in 1865 after serving four years in the Confederate Army. He turned the private stills into a local business, expanding the distillery and selling throughout the Winston-Salem area. Soon after, he took over full operations of the business.

But things really changed when John L. Casper came into the picture. Once old enough, he began an apprenticeship under his father. John L. displayed a real knack for business, in particular, for understanding the power and methodology of advertising.

Max could feel John L.'s anxious desire to run things bleed through every article he read. "Don't do anything stupid, and you'll get the kingdom soon enough."

Luckily for John L., he had the patience to wait. No nefarious or mysterious accidents befell his father, and in the late-1890s, he finally gained control. Moving fast, he put together an investment brochure with the aim of taking the company in a new and profitable direction — mail order liquor.

Max chuckled. "Ambitious little guy."

Ambitious and successful. Investment came in, and with the aid of a few friends and his own finances, John incorporated and for the first time, officially, created The Casper Company. He became president and chief operating officer, and quite quickly, he grew the company by acquiring twenty-one other distilleries in nearby Yadkin and Davie Counties.

While accomplishing all of this, he set up a massive advertising campaign across the nation's newspapers and magazines. He pronounced The Casper Company as the lowest-priced whiskey distributor to be found and the largest mail order business in the entire South. A typical Casper ad touted: "All the North Carolina whiskey we sell is good — there's no bad. People here wouldn't adulterate if they knew how — they are too honest! Most whiskey sellers are noted for mixing, blending and watering. We sell more genuine old whiskey and less water than any known competitor."

As Max scrolled down an article, he knew the man's gambit would succeed. "You push that hard in a world that isn't used to it, and you'll either shine bright or flame out."

John L. shined. By 1905, his company had a net worth of

over $250,000. John used the profits to build what he claimed to be "the largest building in the world devoted to the mail order whiskey trade." Max didn't know if that were true, but the building certainly looked huge. It took up an entire city block in Winston-Salem. Not only did they handle their own whiskey mail order business, but the building also became the local outlet for Milwaukee's Pabst Beer.

Max stepped away from his desk to stretch his back and roll his neck. Dawn would be coming soon enough, and he considered tumbling into bed for a little bit before reading the rest of Casper's life. However, the thought of ascending a flight of stairs that at the moment rivaled Mount Everest kept him from moving.

Instead, he shuffled through the kitchen and entered the half-bath off to the side. Throughout the long night, he hadn't been paying attention to the needs of his body. All the coffee he had swallowed, all the shock he had absorbed, all the nerve-wracking events he had experienced finally added up. He stood at the toilet, listening to his steady stream, unable to do anything more than sigh in relief.

Until he saw the trash can.

Through bleary, dry eyes, he swore he could see a plastic stick poking up through the used tissues — a plastic stick quite similar to a pregnancy test. Despite an entire evening of adrenaline rushing through his body over and again like high tide on a stormy night, he still managed to pump enough of the stuff through his system that he perked up, wide awake, his eyes locked open and staring at the trash. Stone still. Heart racing. Hardly a breath.

Am I going to be a father?

Max flushed the toilet and washed up in the sink. He moved slow and deliberate, trying not to snatch glances at the stick in the trash while also avoiding eye contact with his reflection in the bathroom mirror.

Years ago, they had stopped talking seriously about children. It was always something in the far future, and as time went on, it became something that they both knew would never be. He was okay with that. He knew his mother wanted grandchildren, but his life had never been conducive to child-rearing. Especially after moving to the South and encountering Drummond, the Hulls, and the real world as opposed to the one people think to be real.

Yet right behind him, an alternative life sat atop a nest of tissues. He merely had to pick up that stick and read it.

His hands shook. He stared at them, marveling at the idea that a little piece of plastic could cause such a reaction. Except he couldn't be sure whether he feared looking at the stick or not looking at it.

"Here we go," he whispered. "Count to three and then just check it out. 1 ... 2 ... 3 ..."

In case his body or mind might balk, he moved fast. He whirled around, bent over the trash, and snatched up the plastic stick. Not giving himself any time, he spun the stick until he found the marked window and saw the line — negative. Not pregnant.

Dropping the stick back in the trash, Max let loose a long sigh and collapsed onto the toilet seat. He hadn't felt that kind of a scare since college — nor that kind of intense relief. An involuntary smile crossed his lips. Everything would remain normal.

Except Sandra had been acting strange lately. *Could this be what's been behind her behavior?*

Their entire conversation in the alley sounded quite different under this new light as did her insistence regarding the Darian case. Of the two of them, she had always been the one who wanted kids more. How long had she been sitting on the news that she might be pregnant? All the hoping and dreaming and planning that whipped through her head like a hurricane of never-ending thoughts must have been exhausting. And then to have it all dashed away by a line on a stick.

Max wanted to rush upstairs and hold his wife. He wanted to kiss her, let her know that he loved more than ever, and that he was there for her. Instead, he walked back to his study. If he did go upstairs, if he did say those things, the conversation would have turned toward a question — *Would it have been so bad?* And once that Pandora's Box was opened, they would soon end up discussing purposefully getting pregnant.

"No," Max said to his desk. They had closed those doors already. To open them again would only bring hurt.

As Max delved back into the life of John L. Casper, part of him kept picturing the pregnancy test. Another part of him saw Sandra. And another part chastised him for staying quiet. Risking pain was a necessary part of a good, eventful life. Besides, ignoring this information would only build up walls between him and Sandra, walls they had worked hard to tear down.

He decided to let her sleep. The more rested she was, the better chance they had of getting through this discussion without a fight. She would probably awake in an hour or so. He would talk with her then.

Chapter 10

THE REMAINING TIME UNTIL SUNRISE CREPT BY. Each second clicked upon the wall clock like the ticking bomb in a thriller — Max would count out five seconds passing, but the clock only showed two. When amber light finally slipped into his office, Max had to stop himself from bounding upstairs to question his wife.

Another tense half-hour meandered by before he heard Sandra plodding around. He could tell by the slow thumps of her footsteps that she needed more sleep. She was exhausted, but her body woke every morning at 6:30 no matter what.

When she finally made it downstairs, she poured some coffee and peeked in the study. "Morning, hon," she said, her voice low and cracked. "Had any breakfast yet?"

Max figured the sensitive conversation would go smoother if he waited until she was properly fed and caffeinated. "I'll take care of it. Eggs?"

She smiled and sipped her coffee. Max kissed her as he went to the stove. He fried up four organic eggs, made a few slices of whole wheat toast, and set out artisanal strawberry jam — a simple breakfast they could never have afforded a year ago.

Sandra dug in with vigor. "I feel like I haven't eaten in days."

Nibbling at a piece of toast, Max nodded. He knew he was staring at her, but he couldn't look away. He tried to place his discovery into the context of the woman in front of him, but it all felt foreign.

"Did you find anything out?" she asked, her attention stuck on her food.

Max wanted to burst out laughing. *Did I find anything out?* He imagined her reaction when he threw the pregnancy test onto the table like Zeus hurling a lightning bolt. Then he saw himself sidling next to her and putting his arm around her shoulder. Their heads would touch, and he would mention what he saw in the trash. A third image came to mind — him simply reaching across the table, touching her chin, and giving her a look that said, *I know.*

"Hon? You there?" Sandra said, snapping him back to the moment.

"Sorry. I haven't slept at all. I'm a little out of it."

"Maybe we should both go back to bed. Sleep in for a few hours. Or is something bothering you?"

He opened his mouth, paused, and then told her all he had learned about the blue bottle. Sandra listened intently as he detailed the rise of The Casper Company. Each part of that family's story made it easier to move on to the next and further away from the heavy thoughts weighing his mind.

When he reached the point that Casper built up a whole block of the city, he had managed to clear his head of all but the case. "Things were going great," he said, "and John Casper saw a bright future ahead."

"From the sound of that, I'm guessing things went sour."

"Yup. It started quietly in 1901 with a simple bill passed here in North Carolina requiring all distilleries to be in incorporated towns. Not a big deal, really. More of a nuisance since it forced Casper to relocate some of his operations. The real problem was that Governor Robert Glenn had begun to stir up the anti-alcohol sentiments in people — some say it was for his own political means, but it looks like he really believed in the evils of alcohol. Other laws came out, each one making it more and more difficult for Casper to run his business. Until finally, in 1906, North Carolina became the first state to go completely dry."

"I thought Prohibition was in the 20s."

"Started in 1920. But North Carolina was way ahead of the curve on this one. Casper couldn't fight the state — well, he could've, but it would have been a waste. Too many people were riled up about alcohol and that made the politicians scared. But Casper wasn't going to just roll over, either."

"Of course not. The guy's making serious money, especially for back then. We've both seen enough to know that for people like that, making that much money, it's like a fire burning in their brains."

"Yeah, well, Casper took that idea a bit further. He razed his company to the ground."

"Literally?"

"Almost. He moved the entire business. Every last bit of it. Anything he couldn't take with him, he sold off. The footprint of The Casper Company in Winston-Salem was erased."

"Moved his family, too?"

Max hesitated, the word *family* floating before him, the letters formed from plastic, pregnancy test sticks. Shaking off the image, he said, "Casper never married, never had kids. When he moved, it was just him. He took the company to Roanoke. It's only a few hours north of here, but it's Virginia. Different state, different laws."

"All good until Prohibition."

"Not even that long. Things started out great. Money rolled in and he built on a fourteen acre property. But then it all soured. Not sure why. I suspect the cost of moving everything out of North Carolina and building anew caught up with him. Whatever the case, and here's the first really weird part that I've found, in 1911, he pops up in Florida working with the Atlantic Coast Distillery Company."

"That doesn't sound so weird. What's so special?"“

"At the same time, he was also on record living over a thousand miles away, running the Uncle Sam Distilling Company in Arkansas."

"Okay, that's a bit weird."

"Just a bit. How does a guy who loses everything suddenly have the capital to fund two new companies that are a huge distance apart? It's strange. But then in 1913, the whole thing grinds to a halt. Congress passed the Webb-Kenyon Act, actually overrode a Presidential veto to do it, and that made it illegal to transport alcohol into dry states."

"And that means the post office can't deliver whiskey anymore."

"Exactly. The mail order alcohol business was over. By the time Prohibition became the law everywhere, Casper's life had gone way off-track. In the end, he died somewhere in Mexico, unknown by all but at least living in a country that allowed him to drink."

Sandra cleared their plates and loaded the dishwasher. "That's a wild story. But I'm not sure it really helps us. You said that Casper left Winston-Salem in 1906."

"Right, when the state went dry."

"The Darians' house wasn't built until the 1920s. By that point, Casper's life had crumbled apart. He might even have been heading to Mexico by that time. So what could Casper possibly have to do with the house?"

"I don't know. But if you're some otherworldly spirit and have only one opportunity to send a message to the living, you don't send a blue bottle unless it means something."

Sandra shuddered. "That thing is not right. Even with it all the way in your study, I can feel energy coming off it."

"You mean like magic?"

"Probably. I'm not sure."

Max gazed across the kitchen and into his study. "Maybe you can take the bottle and identify whatever magic's on it."

Sandra closed the dishwasher with a bit too much force. "I'm not a practiced witch. I see ghosts and I understand that world a bit, but you seem to think I can do anything with magic."

"You can do more than me. If we had a witch on payroll, I wouldn't bother you, but that's not the case. So, whatever you can do is better than nothing."

"Other than tell you I can feel energy coming off it, I don't know what I can do."

"But I thought you had gotten interested in the subject. You follow the blogs and websites. You were the one who helped out at Baxter House with the spells."

"Just because I've dabbled, doesn't mean I'm capable of dealing with whatever I'm feeling from that bottle. You want a witch on retainer; you'd be better off finding a new witch. Maybe before she died, Connor had a student."

Max raised an eyebrow. "Would you trust any witch that studied under Connor? She tried to kill us way too many times. Not that one time is okay, but you get my point."

"And that's my point. I'm no witch, and we can't trust a witch. So, be satisfied knowing that the bottle has something going on."

"Hold on." Much like Drummond, Max tapped his chin and pursed his lips as he thought. "We do know a witch — one that's on our side. Sort of. Mother Hope."

"Are you crazy? Those Magi people may not be our enemies, but I wouldn't trust them. And neither would you."

"Who said anything about trust? All I'm saying is that we can use them." Max checked his watch. "We can clean up and be in Greensboro before the morning rush really hits."

"It's a bad idea, and you know it."

"Of course, it's a bad idea. But who else can we go to?"

Sandra brushed by Max on her way toward the stairs. "You can go, but I've got an appointment." Before Max could say a word, she added, "A real appointment. Doctor's appointment."

Though he tried to keep his eyes on Sandra, he snatched a glance at the bathroom trash. "Something wrong?"

She forced a smile. "I'm fine."

Chapter 11

BEFORE TRAVERSING ROUTE 40 to Greensboro and Mother Hope, Max stopped by his office. He went straight to the little corner shop and bought a bagel and a bottle of water. Setting a rapid pace, he walked down the block and into the rundown section of the city. He headed straight for PB's place.

As crazy as the last day had been, PB rumbled in the back of Max's head all the while. Sometimes it was little more than a feeling; sometimes PB's bruised image flashed in his mind. Yet even though he knew he should focus on the Darians, that he should focus on research, that he should focus on Sandra and her pregnancy test, he could not purge the kid from his mind. PB had become a subconscious flicker, a subliminal message flashing during a movie, yet that kid probably thought of Max only when his stomach grumbled in the morning.

As Max navigated around the piles of rubble and trash, he found PB lounging in the shade of a brick wall. "Brought you some breakfast."

PB never bothered looking at Max, but instead, he scrunched his face as if smelling something distasteful. Max set the meager meal across two bricks. He surveyed the area.

"I'm sorry if I caused you any trouble yesterday. I don't see any sign of that guy, Wolf, around."

Hunger beat out pride. PB snatched the bagel and water and turned away, facing the wall. Max's heart dropped. One bad morning and this kid had reverted to an animalistic state.

"C'mon, PB. Who are you going to talk with, if not me?"

"The rats are good company. At least, they're upfront about what they want."

"I don't want anything. I'm only trying to help you out."

Shifting back around, PB guzzled the water and belched. "You want to ease your guilt — for being rich or white or whatever. I don't really care. Every guy like you is guilty about something, and you think by passing a little food my way, you're such a big help. Really making a difference. But you're always going to leave, and I'm always going to be stuck here."

"Doesn't have to be that way."

"Oh, what now? You going to bring me into your home? Is that it? You want me to call you papa and give you lots of hugs?"

"No," Max said, and before he could think, he added, "But you could work for me." He felt the same shock he saw on PB's face. The words hung in the air and neither knew what to do with them.

Finally, PB threw the plastic water bottle at Max's feet. "Get the hell out of here. You ain't going to give me a job. What am I going to do, huh? Answer phones? I'm sure your clients would love to see somebody like me at the desk when they come in."

"What are complaining about? It's better than this, and it'll pay you cash. Besides, you don't even know what I do."

"You look like a cheap lawyer. Ambulance chaser type."

"Really? You think a lawyer can scrap it up like I did yesterday?"

"Don't care. You ain't seriously hiring me and I ain't doing no job. I got all I need, and what I don't got, I can get. You want to keep showing up with breakfast, that's fine. I'm no fool. I'll take your free food. You want to force me into labor, the hell with that."

Though none of this conversation had gone the way Max intended, he had to admit that he felt better overall. He gave a little wave and walked away.

"Hey! Where you going?"

Max paused. "I got a job to do. Got to earn my living."

He walked a few more steps before PB said, "If I want to check out your so-called job, if I want to see if you're legit, where do I find you?"

"A block over."

"What building?"

"Kind of work I do, you should be able to figure that out yourself."

Max left, suppressing a smile. He had a good feeling the next time he saw PB, the young man would be asking for employment. Now, all Max had to do was figure out how they could possibly afford to hire him and what he could possibly do.

About twenty minutes later, Max drove to a gas station and filled up for the trip to Greensboro. Modern country played over the loudspeakers — an ode to drinking hard and falling in love. His mind played ping-pong between his upcoming discussion with Mother Hope and his previous discussion with Sandra.

"You think any harder and smoke's going to come out your ears." Drummond appeared on the opposite side of the car.

Max checked if anybody around could catch him talking to thin air. The only other car sat two pumps over, and the driver had gone inside only moments before. "Did you find anything in the Other?"

"I've searched all over there, put out a few feelers, and nothing. Can't find anybody who died in the house or built the house or anything."

"How's that possible? Those people can't all still be alive. Even someone who built the place at a real young age would be over a hundred by now."

"The Other doesn't house all the dead. It's not as if George Washington is hanging out with Lauren Bacall. It's a place for the ghosts — an alternate plane for those of us who are still here."

"I know. But none of the people who should be connected to the house are there? That's crazy. Somebody should be around."

"They've probably all moved on to whatever comes after. It's possible that one or two are in the Other and hiding, but I can't imagine why that would be. No, my gut tells me that they've all moved on."

Max topped off the gas and recapped the tank. "That doesn't leave us much."

"Just whatever you found out last night at the Darians' house."

Indicating the blue Casper bottle on the passenger seat, Max said, "There's that. The house made a big show of noise and lights and then it left us that."

"Wow, I haven't seen a Casper Blue in a long time."

"You know about that bottle?"

Drummond stuck his face through the side of the car and right up next to the bottle. Though he couldn't smell it, he inhaled anyway. "My father's favorite whiskey. Whenever he could afford it, he'd announce, 'I'm getting me some Casper Blue.' That's what he liked to call it. I don't know if that was a real brand name or anything, but I do recall that it was expensive stuff."

"The ads I found all claimed to be the lowest-priced whiskey around."

"Back when the company was running, sure. By the time my old man was a full-fledged alcoholic, the Casper Company hadn't been around for some time. Finding an unopened blue bottle was a delight, and since each one meant one less in the world, they were expensive."

"Was it worth it?"

Drummond's wistful eyes looked over the bottle once more. "Never had it. My father wasn't about to give his kid a shot of whiskey — especially the expensive stuff. When I got older and gained an appreciation for whiskey, I never found a bottle that I could try. According to my father, though, ol' Casper could sure make a hell of a good drink."

"That's a good idea," Max said, his focus drifting off as his thoughts raced around his head.

"What is?"

"I want you to go back into the Other."

"I told you already, I didn't find anybody. And my sources

will let me know if someone's hiding."

"No, no, forget about all that. I want you to look for John L. Casper."

"Casper?"

"He died somewhere in Mexico and nobody really knows what happened to him. Considering how big The Casper Company became during its heyday, and if you add in the fact that they dealt in whiskey, I'm thinking there's a good chance Casper didn't *move on* with ease. Right? He could be in the Other."

Drummond brought his hands together in one strong clap. "This is why I like working with you. That brain of yours comes up with some clever ideas now and then."

Max started the car and pulled into traffic. "Let me know as soon as you find anything out."

"You got it. So, what about you? Where are you going?"

"Me?" The seatbelt rubbed against Max's neck. He readjusted it but still felt as if it dug into him.

Drummond pointed a finger at him. "You going to answer me or are you going to keep fidgeting like the guiltiest criminal ever to sit in an interrogation room?"

With his face heating up, Max said, "Sorry. I just don't think you're going to like this."

"I already don't like it. So, out with it."

Max explained how Sandra could feel energy pulsing off the bottle, how they didn't have a witch they could use, and that the only option was to take the bottle to Mother Hope.

Drummond flicked the rim of his hat. "That woman is not going to bring you anything but trouble."

"You got a better idea? I don't see another option."

"Unfortunately, you might be right. She'll still cause you trouble, but I don't know how else you'll get the answers. I'd think maybe Leed could help, but he's been pretty quiet since being at the Darians' house. He's still with me, but he's not the same."

Max eased along the Route 40 on-ramp. "I'll be in Greensboro in about twenty-thirty minutes. You come up with something better before then, please tell me. Otherwise, go find Casper."

Drummond faced Max with a grave look. Usually, his ghostly temperature didn't bother Max or even register, but this time, Max could feel the air in the car chilling around him. "You be real careful," Drummond said, each word dropping the temperature faster. "Never forget that she's a witch. The Magi group may be on our side — at least, most of the time — but no matter what Mother Hope says, she's still a witch."

"I know. Don't worry."

"And above all else, don't you dare promise her anything. You understand? Don't make any promises."

"All I want is for her to check out this bottle. That's it. I'm not going to let our conversation go down any other avenue. And if she won't help me out, then so be it. I'll thank her for her time, get back on the road, and come home. It'll —"

Drummond snapped out a finger and pointed at Max's face. "Don't you dare say it'll be easy."

"I wasn't going to."

Of course, Max had lied.

Chapter 12

STANDING IN THE SHADOW of the brick and granite O. Henry Hotel, Max tried to shuck off the sense of dread driving down his shoulders. Hard to do when the last time he had stepped foot in this place, he nearly lost his life.

"You sure there isn't another witch?" Max muttered to the parking lot. When no answer came, he trudged up to the lobby.

The place had not changed. The dark wood walls, high ceilings, and overwhelming smell of a fireplace gave the hotel a dignified and stuffy aura as if at any moment, British gentlemen from the 19th century would enter smoking cigars and swirling cognac. The brass elevators on his right and the classy reception desk on his left broke the illusion but not by much.

A short walk ahead, the wide lobby opened into a large sitting room. Thick, heavy furniture created a miniature labyrinth and classical music swept around the area, floating up to the ceiling two stories above. And, of course, the most important part of the hotel rested near that ceiling — O. Henry's famous short story, *The Gift of the Magi*, had been painstakingly painted in one long spiraling path covering all four walls. It looked like an artistic homage of the hotel to its namesake, but Max knew better. Those words acted as runes to a spell that formed a protective barrier around the building. Not protecting Max, of course, but rather the witch he intended to see.

Since nobody bothered to greet him, Max approached the reception desk. A man and a woman worked at the desk. The woman busied herself with her computer while the man picked up a phone and spoke in a low tone. Neither smiled at him or welcomed him or even offered to help him. The suspicious way they eyed him suggested all he needed to know.

Instead of talking with them, Max turned toward the lounge area and plunked down on an overstuffed couch. And he waited. His eyes felt heavy. He had been up for over twenty-four hours, and the idea of a quick rest pushed him deeper into the couch.

He knew they watched him. Even with his eyes closed, he could feel it. But even if that detective's sense for danger hadn't been improving, simple logic told him that the Magi group would never allow their leader and witch to be anywhere that wasn't under surveillance. Only a short time later, he heard footsteps approaching. He forced his eyes open and saw two broad-chested men wearing ill-fitting suits.

With a low groan, Max got to his feet. "If you two aren't the muscle around here, I'll have to go buy a hat just so I can eat it."

One of the men had a pencil-thin goatee. His square head blocked out his partner. "Is there something we can help you with?"

"I'm here to see Mother Hope."

"Concerning what?"

"That's for Mother Hope."

Square-head grinned as if Max's stubbornness would make his day. "Nobody gets to see her without declaring their intentions."

"My intentions? Gentlemen, I'm not interested in marrying the woman. I simply have a question for her. I'm sure if you let her know that Max Porter is here, she'll see me."

To his partner, Square-head said, "Everybody thinks they're special." The partner snickered.

"I'm not saying I'm special. It's simply that Mother Hope and I have had some past dealings. She knows who I am and will, at least, hear me out."

Square-head's voice turned grim. "About what?"

"About none of your damn business. Now, I understand you've got a job to do, but you need to understand that your boss deals with sensitive information and I'm not about to tell just anyone —"

Square-head grabbed Max's hand and twisted it in such a way that Max spun around. His wrist burned and his elbow locked. Square-head's partner chuckled as Square-head continued to speak in a calm but menacing tone. "We understand our jobs perfectly. You want to see her? Then come with us."

With a push of the arm, Max had no choice but to stumble forward. Trying to stand his ground would only result in breaking his arm. "I'm moving. Let me go and I'll keep moving."

Square-head maintained his control of Max's arm. He turned Max down a hall and into a private elevator. If anybody witnessed this assault, they chose not to offer help. At least, Square-head released Max's arm once the elevator started to descend.

To avoid making eye contact with either thug, Max watched the display above the door. When the elevator eased to a stop, the display read B4. On the floor selection panel, there were buttons for the Lobby (L) and the floor below (B1), but none other after that. No B2 or B3, and certainly no B4.

The elevator doors slid open, revealing a dismal hall with a wood-slat door on each side — one close to the elevator, the second about halfway down the corridor — and one metal door at the end. They stopped at the second wood-slat door. Square-head shoved Max inside.

Max had expected the sparse room to have a two-way mirror much like a police interrogation room, and the Magi group did not disappoint. However, he did not expect the absence of a table and chairs. Most certainly, he had no inkling that the wall opposite the mirror would bear two thick, metal rings — the kind used for prisoners in medieval dungeons.

"Perhaps we've got off on the wrong foot," Max said.

As he broke for the door, his gut met with Square-head's solid fist. The air rushed out of Max's lungs as his stomach slammed up against its neighboring organs. With his legs weakening, Max groped for the wall to keep from falling over. Square-head's friend, the one who kept chuckling, rushed in and smashed his shoulder against Max's.

"Don't break his bones," Square-head said.

Chuckles hocked up in his mouth and spit on the floor. "You gotta let me do more than that. C'mon. I been waiting for this."

"Tie him up for now."

Chuckles knotted one meaty hand in Max's shirt and thrust him against the wall. "I'd love for me a reason to pound your skull, so give me a hard time. Please."

Max opted to put his energy into standing. As his legs regained their strength — at least, a modicum of strength — he noticed Square-head locking the door. Chuckles continued to earn his name as he used coarse rope to tie Max's wrists to the iron rings in the wall.

"What's that?" Square-head stepped across the room to where Max had fallen. From the floor, he lifted the blue bottle. He pressed the bottle against Max's cheek. "What's with this? You got poison in here or something?"

"Poison? There's no top on the bottle." Max knew Chuckles would punch him for being snide, but he couldn't stop himself.

"Answer my partner," Chuckles said and did as expected.

Max clamped down his jaw, hoping to avoid throwing up. Not only would that signal weakness to his captors, but he feared what they might do should he accidentally hit them with his vomit.

Square-head pushed the bottle harder into Max's face. "Not poison. Perhaps a spell, then?"

Seeing Chuckles ready to punch again, Max's body dropped in defeat. No point in going on when these two would clearly keep beating him for nothing. "Rein in your dog."

"He talking about me?" Chuckles said.

"Easy. I think he's ready. That right? You going to tell me what this bottle is about?"

"I don't know. Really. I came here to show that bottle to Mother Hope. I think there's a spell around it or connected to it or something, and I want her help to discover what's so special about it. That's it. That's why I'm here."

Square-head hesitated. Max could see the dismay on the man's face. He may have been counting on a more serious threat to Mother Hope. Perhaps saving her life from a sneaky assassin would have garnered him great praise or a promotion. But Max's words must have sounded true — not only because they were true but because Max's emphatic tones suggested the real panic that threatened to set in. Max was scared and Square-head knew it.

To Chuckles, he said, "Come on. Let's check this out."

Square-head left with the bottle in hand. Chuckles glanced back. "Stay here," he said, snickering as he walked out.

Max didn't bother straining against his bonds. He already knew they were tight. Instead, he flexed his fingers, hoping to keep some circulation going through.

When the door opened, he braced for another beating. Leon entered and closed the door with a soft touch. The dim lighting of the room made it hard to see all of Leon's features, but Max could see enough — pity mixed with worry. Neither emotion appeared to be on Max's behalf.

Standing with his back to the mirror, Leon said, "I told you not to come here, that you would only cause trouble."

"I thought you people looked into me. Don't you know I'm always causing trouble?"

"There's nothing for you to gain here. When they come back, apologize and get the hell out of here."

Max clicked his tongue. "I think I'll stay."

"They might hurt you more."

"Been my experience that when the beatings start, I'm usually on the right track."

"*Usually* is the operative word. This time, you're wrong."

Something in Max's side dug hard. He hoped they hadn't broken one of his ribs. "Look, I'm not trying to screw you over. If I had an alternative, I wouldn't have come here. Untie me, and I'm sure we can work this out."

"You think I'm here to help you? I was helping you when I

told you not to come."

"Bullshit," Max said — if Leon wouldn't help him, at least the guy would be stuck with a guilty conscience. "You said that for yourself. You pawned this case off on me, cut out the only witch who I'd dare to ask for help, and now you don't want to be held responsible."

Leon stormed to the door and stopped with his hand on the knob. "I'm going to tell you what to do. You listen and do what I say, and you'll get out of here alive — bruised but breathing, and definitely not cursed. You ignore me, and I won't be responsible. Not for any of it."

"Whatever makes you sleep at night."

Leon glowered at Max. He gripped the knob tighter as if strangling Max instead of a piece of metal. "Mother Hope will agree to see you. When she does, you ask her only what you really came here for. Don't let the conversation wander off. She'll try. You keep things focused. Get your answer and get out as fast as possible. Whatever you do, do not promise her anything."

"That's it?"

"That's enough. Do what I said and you'll be fine."

"Piece of advice in return — you shouldn't be involved with people you're this scared of."

"Mother Hope does good work. We're fighting the Hulls and that's worth a bit of fear on my part. Besides, I know how to handle myself with her. My being scared — that's for you."

Leon left. Alone and feeling the bite of rope against his wrists, Max swore the room darkened and grew colder. His brave face peeled away. A tremble worked its way up from his legs.

He waited.

For how long, he had no idea. Could have been fifteen minutes. Could have been an hour or two. He only knew that, despite his efforts, his hands had gone numb, and his back ached from being stuck in the same position. Only that pain kept him awake.

When the door finally opened again, Chuckles entered with

a hunting knife — any bigger and the thing would have been a machete. The lug moved in, licking his lips as he waved the knife under Max's throat.

Max had hoped to keep a stoic face — give nothing to this brute. But the way Chuckles laughed told Max he had failed. Then he felt his jaw quivering.

"Don't wet yourself," Chuckles said. "I ain't gonna kill you. I'd like to, but Mother Hope wants to see you." With the knife, he cut the ropes binding Max's hands. "You do anything stupid, and maybe afterwards I'll get a chance."

With a rough hand, Chuckles gripped Max by the upper arm and pushed him out of the room. Square-head waited in the hall.

Max knew to keep quiet, but his mouth opened anyway. "Told you she'd want to see me."

Square-head ignored Max's cocky look and gestured toward the elevators. Chuckles, however, smacked the back of Max's head. "Shut up and walk."

Max obeyed.

The elevator rode all the way to the top floor. Only the fifth floor, but the penthouse suite nonetheless. The entire trip up, Chuckles squeezed tighter. Max knew he'd have finger-shaped bruises on his arm for the next week. Hopefully, it wouldn't get any worse.

Growing up, Max had learned not to make too many assumptions about people. His time with Drummond had taught him that often a detective had to make assumptions. As they entered the suite, Max drew some pretty quick assumptions that he had to gamble would be correct.

First, he decided this suite did not belong to Mother Hope. Everything about the place spoke to a modern, stylish flair. Black marble floors with white, sparse furniture. Huge flatscreen on one wall and Japanese prints on the opposite. The only color burst from a lavish floral arrangement sitting in the middle of a black block coffee table. Nothing about this place agreed with Mother Hope.

She was an old woman who dressed like an older gypsy and

carried with her none of the light, airy feel of the suite. An aura of dark surrounded her, brought on by the strange, cursed things she had seen and experienced over her lifetime. At least, for the moment, she used her abilities as a witch to fight against the magic of people like the Hull family. But Max would not count on that.

Square-head stopped at the doorway. Chuckles thrust Max forward and then took up position next to his partner.

"Please, Mr. Porter, sit and be welcome."

In the corner to Max's left, Mother Hope rested in a white armchair. The blue Casper bottle stood on a black cylinder meant to be a side table. Max lowered to the edge of the couch.

"You want me to tell you about this bottle." Mother Hope's inflection had no question in it.

"I already know about the bottle. I want you to tell me about the spell or whatever magic is on the bottle."

She grinned and the wrinkles in her face flattened. "Is this for one of your cases?"

"That's not really important." Max remembered everything Leon had said. He had to keep the conversation focused on the answers he sought. Nothing else. Besides, Max had no intention of betraying Leon, so the less said the better.

"Perhaps you'll tell me where or how you came into possession of the bottle."

"Again, not important. I only want to know about the magic."

Mother Hope folded her arms and peeked at the bottle. "You are not being too helpful. More insulting, you are not being too observant. Either that or you're simply rude."

"I don't know what I missed, but I guarantee I have no desire to be rude."

"Surely, one who claims to be a detective would notice that I am not the same decrepit old woman he had met before."

The moment she said the words, Max saw it. She looked several years younger, more vibrant, less wrinkled, perhaps even stronger. But he had to put that out of his thoughts. Stay focused.

"I guess you've got some powerful mojo," he said. "I'd be grateful if you'd use some of it on the bottle now."

"Mojo? How quaint. The ability to cast off years is not some mere trickery. It is among the most difficult of spells. Do you want to know how I achieved it?"

"I want you to look at the bottle."

"I succeeded because of that bottle."

Max paused. "Excuse me?"

"In order to gain even a few years of youth, a witch must siphon off energy from an item already imbued with magic. Most items that have been cursed or favored don't have enough energy, and so the spell fails. But this bottle is overflowing. A spell that should have taken a full hour, I pulled off in fifteen minutes. And look at the results."

"Yes, you don't look a day over sixty-five."

A scowl flashed across Mother Hope's face and disappeared. "Not bad for a woman nearing triple digits."

"I suppose. But so far, all you've told me is that the bottle has a lot of magic on it. I already knew that. I want to know what that magic is, why the bottle appeared —"

"It appeared?" Mother Hope's hand shot to the arms of her chair as if bracing for an assault.

Max locked his mouth shut. Stupid. After a slow breath, he said, "I've already spent too much time here, and I can't say I was happy about the welcome I received."

"I won't apologize. My men may be rough, but they protect me from constant threats."

"I want to know if you'll tell me about the magic on the bottle. Yes or no?"

"Well, now, that depends."

"On what?"

"If you're willing to make me a small promise."

There it was. Even if he hadn't been warned, the lust on her lips would have been enough to ring the alarms in his brain. She observed every motion he made, her eyes darting between his hands, his mouth, his legs, his mouth, his eyes, his mouth. Yearning for him to speak the words she needed.

"Sure," he said. "What do you want?" In his head, Max could hear Drummond cursing and screaming.

"A simple matter. All I ask is for you to promise me that you do not go back to the house where you found this bottle. If it's part of a case, then you'll have to recuse yourself. For that, I will take the time to investigate your bottle, and I will report to you what I learn within the week. Sooner, most likely."

Max popped to his feet. "You already know, don't you?"

"The magic? No. Though I have my suspicions."

"You know something about this. It's been right on your face this whole time."

"Oh, bless your heart, you think you can outwit me. Dear, I'm an old, old woman. I've been living here for a long time. Of course I know a lot about a lot that goes on around here. Why should that be a surprise? But information is valuable, and I haven't survived this long by giving it away freely."

"Now what do you want?"

She licked her index finger and made a mark in the air. "I already have you for one promise. That's enough. Leave. I'll contact you when I understand what has been done to this bottle."

Square-head and Chuckles moved forward, but Max put out his hands. "Easy, fellas. I can walk out on my own."

Though they followed him all the way out of the O. Henry Hotel's lobby, neither one placed another hand on him. He got in his car and started back to Winston-Salem and the Darians' house. He had made a promise to help them. He had made that same promise to his wife. In his book, those superseded anything he said to an old witch.

Besides, how would she know what he did unless she had him followed? He checked his rearview mirror. Clear. Over the next minute, he checked it ten more times.

Chapter 13

ROUTE 40 DRIFTED BY, a constant blur of trees, cars, and construction. The last day had become a blur, too. Too many decisions hung above him, waiting for him to place his neck in their noose.

He had to make that promise; otherwise, Mother Hope would have refused to help. It was simple. But he knew nobody would accept his logic — especially Drummond. Considering how little sleep he'd had, perhaps Drummond was right.

Max's cell phone chirped. He answered it before bothering to look at the caller ID. "Hello?"

"Max? I'm so glad I caught you." His mother. Great — from one mother to the next. "How are you doing?"

"I'm fine, Mom."

"Uh-oh. You don't sound so fine. What's wrong?"

"Nothing to be worried about. Just the day to day stuff."

"Come on, now. You're talking with your mother. I've been learning to hear your tones since you were born and could only cry when you needed your diaper changed. Now, what's the matter?"

Usually, Max could deflect her with ease. Of course, this would be the time his mother decides to dig in. But what could he say? He didn't want to lie to her, but she would never believe that he had troubles brewing with a witch, a ghost, an unknown spell, and a haunted house. In fact, if Max said any of that, his mother would probably take the first flight to North Carolina and have him committed.

His mouth solved the problem by blurting out the first thing he thought of that she could understand and accept. "Well, I found a pregnancy test and —"

"You're having a baby?" Max could practically hear the fireworks bursting out of her.

"No, Mom. The test was negative. But Sandra's been acting a bit odd lately."

With a knowing laugh, Max's mother said, "This is what you're confused about? Men. You all are so thick sometimes. Your father was one of the worst. I could write him a note that I wanted to travel for my birthday, and he'd buy me a diamond, saying he had no idea what to get me."

"At least, we know where I get it from. You want to clue me in to why she's upset?"

"It's obvious, dear. She wants a baby."

Max shook his head. "I know you want her to want to have a baby, but I'm not so sure. Last time we talked about it, she seemed scared of being pregnant."

"Of course, she's scared. It's frightening enough the first time around but think about her age. She's no young, little thing. That can cause complications. I'm sure it's got to be quite conflicting in her head. She wants to have a baby but fears losing it because her womb is getting old, yet she's running out of time to have children."

"Maybe, but —"

"Listen to me. I know these things. She may have spent many years crowing about how she never wanted kids, but all women have the desire for children. It's in our blood. Just takes some a bit longer to recognize it."

Max tried to ignore this last jibe and focused on the overall idea. Sandra had been so vehement about the Darian case — particularly about protecting Shawnee Darian's unborn child. Maybe his mother was right. Maybe Sandra felt her biological clock winding down and this case had brought it all crashing to the forefront. It would explain most of her behavior lately.

"Oh, this is going to be wonderful," his mother said. "You let me know when the timing's right, and I'll make sure to help you outfit this baby proper. You'll need a crib and a changing table. And diapers! You'll need lots of those."

"Mom, calm down. Sandra's not even pregnant yet."

"But she will be. And that'll make me a Grandma. What do you think I should be called? Grandma, Nanna, or Granny? No, not Granny."

Max had to endure for several more minutes before he could extricate himself from the phone call. Once he set aside his cell, he conjured a clear image of Sandra with a full belly of baby sticking out far. She beamed bright as she rubbed her stomach. Pregnancy would certainly look good on her.

And me? he wondered. *How am I going to handle all of this?*

After a moment of thought, and with the naive confidence every first time parent experiences before the baby actually arrives, he decided he could do it, no problem. He could be a father. He could handle that. It might require a few changes in their lives, but so what? If Sandra needed to have a child, he would be on board with the decision.

He smirked as a new thought hit him — their child would have a unique upbringing. Uncle Drummond would be a part of the experience. No way would a child born from him and Sandra not be able to see ghosts. That would bring some challenges in dealing with other children, but Sandra had been through it herself. Surely, she would have a better idea of what to say and how to handle it all.

Max shivered. Like his mother, he was planning for things that were far off — especially because Sandra was not pregnant. Not yet.

She seemed to want to be, and Max now wanted it, too. As he exited the highway and navigated the few roads to the Darians' house, he decided he would broach the subject the first time they were alone. Sandra needed to know she had his support.

Parking the car, he felt some of his stress lifting away. Until he saw Wayne Darian pacing on the front lawn, muttering to himself, and twisting his bottom lip. The blood had drained from his face, and his eyes were wide and darting around.

When he finally spied Max, he called out, "Please, you've got to help us."

Chapter 14

MAX SAUNTERED ACROSS THE STREET and onto the front lawn, knowing he had to deal with Wayne Darian and fed up with the day already. Wayne's head flew to attention as he heard Max approach. He looked like a blind date who thought he had been stood up but suddenly saw a beautiful woman arrive.

And I'm the woman, Max thought. *Sheesh.*

"You okay there, Wayne?"

A sheen of sweat covered Wayne's body. "You've got to help me."

"That's what we're trying to do. You look a little agitated. Something happen?"

With his middle finger, Wayne pointed back at his house with his arm extended so tight, the muscles vibrated. "That Libby woman came back and she's inside there right now interviewing my Shawnee."

"That's to be expected."

"Shawnee's already been interviewed. How many more times does Libby have to ask the same questions? This isn't a police interrogation for crying out loud. You people are supposed to be here to help us."

"I know it's tough. But you understand why that happens? With the police, I mean. Do you understand why they ask the same thing over and over?"

"Because they're trying to trip you up. Catch you in a lie. But we're not lying."

Max made sure to speak slow and calm. Anything to temper Wayne's frazzled mind. "That's true when they interrogate a suspect. But sometimes they're asking questions of a witness, of somebody who saw a crime happen. And when they do that, if given the chance, they'll ask the same questions over and over because when you experience something intense, it can take several times before you really can recall everything. Libby's in there hoping to get some new piece of information that Shawnee had previously not remembered. That's all."

"Well, maybe. But I'm telling you, for all the talking you people do, nothing's getting better around this place."

"I know. I wish we could clear this all up much faster."

Wayne's chin quaked. "It's not fair. All we're trying to do is have a good life down here. We didn't ask for any of this."

Max wondered how long Wayne could hold onto his denial, how long he could pretend the threats to his family had reasonable explanations. Up until this point, Max saw in Wayne's eyes and the way the man spoke that he had not fully accepted his new reality. Part of him must have dismissed it as his wife's imagination. He probably figured he would play along, hire the paranormal investigators, and chalk it all up to some weird experience they could laugh about years later. But now reality crashed upon his head.

Max remembered when he first met Drummond. It had been a terrifying moment in his life. At the time, he had nobody to confide in. Until he learned of Sandra's gifts, he thought himself alone. If nothing else, he could be there for Wayne.

"Look, why don't you join me. I'm going to walk through the house again."

"What good will that do?"

"I'm hoping to find anything I missed before. Nothing to worry about. You come with me, and then you can see the things I see. Maybe you'll even find something important. You'll be helping to fight this thing."

Like a defeated foe, Wayne bowed his head. "Yeah, okay. But what're you looking for?"

"Anything to connect this house with a dead person. While Libby's in there trying to get more details from your wife as to the exact experience she's been going through, I'm here to look into the history of this place. Find out more about it. Find out what specific event happened in the past that is causing this problem today."

"How do you know it has anything to do with the past?"

"I've never heard of a haunting that didn't involve a dead person. And dead people, by definition, come from the past."

Wayne snorted out a short laugh. "I suppose so."

Max led the way through the living room and into Ghost Watching Central aka the kitchen. Libby and Shawnee sat at the equipment cluttered table. Libby clacked away at a laptop as Shawnee answered her questions. They both tossed inquisitive looks at Max and Wayne.

"Don't mind us," Max said. "Just passing through."

With Wayne following, he brought them downstairs to the basement. His previous tour through the house had glossed over this spot, but with all that had happened, Max thought it deserved a more thorough investigation.

Under the sparse brown lighting, Max meandered up and down the wood-shelved aisles. The mold and dust had increased since the previous visit, and a new odor had been added. Five rusting cans with dried paint dribbled down the sides — white, aqua, brown, black, and mustard. One can lacked a top, and a quick peek at the separated oil and pigment showed Max what had produced the strong odor.

From the bottom of the stairs, Wayne said, "Do you really think whatever you're looking for is down here?"

"Would be a good bet. A bunch of this stuff came with the house, right?"

"Everything but the washer and dryer. We brought those in."

Max halted. "*None* of this is yours?"

"I don't think so."

Max stomped up the aisle flailing his arms at various objects. "How could none of this be yours? I get the paint or the rusting screws, but you're saying *none* of it. Not that birdhouse or maybe those warped LPs. None of that stuff belongs to you?"

"No. None of it."

"Only the washer and dryer? What about that stack of clothes on the floor next to the dryer?"

Wayne edged away from the stairs, his face paling with each step. "How did that get here?"

Max followed Wayne's gaze. On top of the clothes pile, a blanket had been partially spread out. The hair on Max's arms stood up. He didn't like the shape the blanket formed — too much like a child underneath. He didn't like the bits of red yarn poking out the back — too much like a doll's hair.

"Do you know what's under that blanket?"

Wayne moved his head from side to side.

Max approached the pile.

Please don't be a clown. Please don't be a clown.

He never had a fear of clowns, but he had seen enough horror movies to know how terrifying a possessed child's toy could be. And none could be more twisted and psychotic looking than the forced happiness on a clown's face.

"That's not right," Wayne said. "That shouldn't be here."

"What's under the blanket?"

But Wayne's jaw moved without any sound.

Max reached out but froze before touching the blanket. If it turned out to be a clown doll, he could handle it. He wouldn't like it, but he could handle it. He'd be waking with night terrors for the next several years, but he would manage. If the thing moved, however, if its eyes looked up at him, or its twisted smile grew, Max would be scrambling for the stairs, screaming nonsense.

He wished Drummond were here. Drummond would know right away what lay under the blanket.

But Drummond's smart enough not to be here. Man, I'm such an idiot.

Wayne would be of no help. Max couldn't ask for Shawnee's help, either. Even if she wasn't pregnant, clearly whatever caused all this trouble had put its focus upon her. That left Libby. No way would Max ask for her help. Her smug satisfaction outweighed his fears. Like pulling off an old bandage, he thrust his hand out and yanked off the blanket.

A pillow.

Just a throw pillow with red fringe.

Hearing both relief and anger in his own voice, Max said, "Damn, that got the better of me."

Wayne had silently come right behind Max and dropped to his knees. The man's hands groped for the blanket.

Pressing the blanket against his nose, Wayne engulfed the scent. "It still smells the same."

"This? This blanket is the big deal?"

Wayne raised his head as tears trailed down his cheeks. "This belonged to my sister."

"Your sister?"

"Charlotte."

Based on Wayne's reaction, Max held little doubt that Charlotte had left the world of the living. "What happened?"

As Wayne continued to stare up at Max, his fingers pilled the edge of the blanket. "I was eight when my mother got pregnant. She and Dad had always planned on it being just me. But she seemed really happy. She'd call me in every night and let me put my ear to her belly so I could listen to the baby grow. And once she found out she was having a little girl, they named her Charlotte and they bought this blanket.

"Every night, I'd go in there and I'd listen and I'd feel her stomach growing. Once the baby started to kick and I could see those strange motions on my mom's skin as the baby's hands and feet pushed out, that was when they brought out the blanket. My mom would wrap it around her stomach at night and she'd tell me it would be like the baby held the blanket. Soon, she promised, the blanket would smell like the baby. When it was time for me to go to bed, she would hand me the blanket and I'd spend my nights with that thing on my pillow, smelling the baby that would soon by my sister.

"I think my mom did all that to help me accept this new life. It wasn't like I was three years old and gaining a sibling that I would grow up with. I was eight. An eight year difference is huge, and I was used to being an only child. I think she really feared I'd have a lot of trouble. But she was wrong.

"I loved the idea of having a sister. I loved the idea of being a big brother and protecting her. The way my mom let me participate in the growth of this baby only strengthened my resolve. I remember one night thinking *Lord, help the sucker who tries to get in my sister's pants when she's a teen. I'll knock his block off.*

"I think it would have been wonderful. But then, my dad started to change. He'd been a good guy all my life up until then. Real father-of-the-year kind of material. But with Charlotte on the way, things changed. Now, I can look back and see that he thought that Charlotte wasn't his. I don't know why, but that's what he thought. And it soured him.

"It all grew out of little things — picking on the noise I made on my plate while eating or forgetting to take out the garbage or not helping my mom pick up a box. Anything. Any little thing he could snap at me about, he did. And if he wasn't snapping at me, he was getting on my mom's case.

"I remember several nights listening to Charlotte grow while Mom made excuses for Dad. She'd tell me that he was anxious about the baby, stressed out about work, about finding the money to pay for this new addition — that sort of thing.

"I believed it at first. At least, I think I did. But then the bruises started showing up. On her face and her arms. At that point, I suspected the truth, but I was too young to really know what was going on. Until that morning ... I wanted to watch Saturday morning cartoons with a bowl of cereal and a glass of orange juice. I remember carrying it to the television. The bowl balanced in one hand, the glass in the other, but I filled the bowl too high with milk. I lost my balance. I tried to save the bowl but that meant letting go of the glass. Everything dropped and shattered.

"My father thundered downstairs. He saw the mess and he lost it. He hit me so hard, I had a swollen lip, a black eye, and bruises along my side. That's when I knew what he had become."

Max withheld his comments. Wayne did not appear aware of his surroundings anyway. He probably would not have heard a word Max said.

"My mom had been a large woman to begin with, and the baby only ballooned her up more. Somewhere around the sixth or seventh month, Dad started in about her weight. Threatening her, telling her she had to lose it all once the baby came or she'd be hearing it from him. I could see the fear in her eyes when she tried to hide it from me.

"But every night, when she'd call me in and it was just the two of us — oh, the love we shared for Charlotte. Holding this blanket against Mom's belly and talking about all the cute things babies do and getting more excited by the day.

"Then one night, he came home — angry, maybe a bit drunk. The fight started before the front door closed — yelling, screaming. I was upstairs. I knew the sounds. I knew what it meant. But something felt different, sounded harsher, crueler."

Wayne's hard stare filled with tears that formed a constant river down his face, dripping off his chin and onto the blanket.

"I was eight. I didn't know what to do. I ran into their bedroom and I grabbed Charlotte's blanket and I ran back to my room and hid in the closet. I sat under that blanket all night long. I heard them yelling through the walls. I could hear the punches, too. All night long. And all I could do was sit there and cry, surrounded by the smell of this blanket."

Wayne grew quiet. He sniffled and rubbed at his eyes. At length, in a soft whisper as if talking to a baby, he added, "Next morning, it was over. No more Charlotte."

Once more, he lifted the blanket to his face and inhaled. But with abrupt force, he threw the blanket down. "What the hell is this? This isn't Charlotte's."

Max saw that the blanket was no blanket at all. Rather, a large oily rag lay lumped on the basement floor. He closed his eyes. *Damn.* He hated these kinds of tricks.

Nudging Wayne with his knee, Max said, "Come on. Let's go upstairs. Get out of this place."

Even as Wayne kept his eyes locked on the rag, he nodded and struggled to his feet. Max clasped Wayne's elbow, assisting him up the stairs. Libby and Shawnee had left the kitchen, and for that, Max was thankful. He didn't want to explain to either of them why Wayne looked so distraught.

He planned to take Wayne outside for fresh air, but Wayne backed up at the front door. "Let's go upstairs. You need to see the rest of the house, don't you?"

"I can do that later," Max said, using Wayne's elbow to direct him toward the front door.

"No. This thing has to stop. My wife can't wait for you all to feel better — or me, for that matter. Let's go upstairs and find whatever you need."

As Wayne ascended the staircase, Max considered calling him back. Outside, they would have a chance to recompose. Max had dealt with enough of magic and the otherworldly to know when the situation had turned for the worse. The thing haunting this house lacked all subtlety and had attacked too many times to be thought of as anything less than hostile.

Attacking Wayne through his memories, assaulting Drummond and Sandra with a sonic blast, shaking the house to its core — all signs of a spirit suffering far beyond simple anger. This enraged thing needed fear and negativity surrounding it. Its actions showed it would do everything it could manage to foster those feelings.

The bottle — Max looked at his phone. Mother Hope might be in danger if that bottle was infused with something evil.

"You coming?" Wayne called from upstairs.

Mother Hope could handle herself. Max needed to watch out for Wayne. Besides, the only way he could help this family was to find something to connect this house to a significant death.

As he clumped up the stairs, he whispered, "Only way is through."

When Max reached the top, Wayne called from a room. "I'm in here. Where all the action takes place."

Max didn't like the sound of Wayne's voice. It had a smarmy quality that didn't belong in the man's mouth. Walking down the hall, Max peeked in the baby's room, but it was empty. Further down, he reached the master bedroom. He found

Wayne sitting on the corner of a king-sized bed.

Wayne looked surprisingly chipper, as if nothing had occurred in the basement. With his bright smile, he waved Max in and patted a spot on the bed next to him. "Have a seat, pal."

"Hard to look around if I'm sitting."

Wayne wagged his finger. "Oh, you're a clever one." He gave the bed a short bounce. "I'm telling you, if this bed could talk — oh boy, the stories it would tell. Just me and my wife, but man, that woman's a tiger. I guess when she's old, she'll be a cougar."

Max cracked an obligatory grin.

"What about your wife? Sandra? She's a hottie. What's she like in bed?"

Having been through the possession of his own wife, Max's first thoughts led him along a similar path. Perhaps the attack in the basement had done more than rattle Wayne. Perhaps it had opened him up, made him vulnerable to whatever entity they faced in this house.

Except, Wayne did not behave anything like Sandra had during her possession. Obviously, his drastic change in behavior was odd, but it could have been a defensive reaction to his memories. Overcompensating with bawdy joy in an effort to tamp down his dark thoughts. When he got a chance, Max would have to ask Sandra and Drummond to take a closer look at Wayne.

Throwing his arms about, Wayne said, "You going to look around or not?"

Max poked around the room and checked the closets. "I think I'm more interested in the baby's room."

Upon hearing the word *baby*, Wayne's eyes clouded and his mouth dropped. In a monotone, he said, "Sure. Let's go check the baby's room."

Max returned up the hall, not happy having Wayne behind him. Once inside the baby's room, he did his best to blot out Wayne's behavior. He had to focus on searching with care. On hands and knees, he inspected the baseboards, looking for anything he could consider a clue. When he checked the closet, he spied an access panel in the ceiling.

"You have an attic?"

Wayne shrugged. "I think it's a crawl space. I don't know. Never went up there."

"Get me a chair or a step-stool or something."

Wayne left, and Max watched the access panel for any movement. When Wayne returned with a chair, Max got up, popped the access panel, and hauled himself into the windowless attic. "Why can't somebody ever haunt a bright, cheery room?" To Wayne, he added, "Is there a light switch down there for this?"

A moment later, a single bare bulb flicked on. Wayne's hands gripped the sides of the entrance and he pulled himself up.

The attic rivaled the basement in clutter. Mounds of old newspapers and magazines rose from floor to angled ceiling like ancient chimneys. Several paintings had been stacked at one side. Max saw mirrors and drawers and other pieces of incomplete furniture. Three wooden boxes had been stacked to the right. Dust covered every object. Shadows covered more.

Wayne drew a smiley face in the dust. "Man, a person could drown in the stuff the previous owners left behind. They must've been real hoarders."

Max got to work. Coughing as he sifted through one dusty bin after another, he found objects from various decades. Newspapers mostly had dates from the 1940s. Several books in one crate were copies of Dickens, 1930s editions. He even found a woman's lace gloves. Based on the slim, childlike size, he knew it dated to the 1920s.

As Max continued his search, Wayne sneezed three times. "I'm telling you. This place is nothing but a big mistake. Shawnee and I ought to sell it, move on, and be done."

"I wouldn't blame you for wanting to get out of this. But you can't just go selling it."

"What do you mean? Why not?"

"Well, it's not like there's a state law against it, but there's a moral law that you shouldn't do it. Or it'd be like selling poisoned food at a restaurant. You know whoever moves in here next will have problems too."

"I don't know anything of the kind. I don't even know what's really happening here."

Max held his tongue and continued his search. He tried to stay focused on the present task, but a thought struck him and he couldn't hold it back. "You know, we found nothing to connect this entity to the house."

"So?"

"If you move, it might just follow you."

"It can do that?"

"The world of ghosts is a lot more complex than a bunch of bedtime stories."

Wayne's eyes lowered, and his lips tightened into a mean, heartless line. "Then you better hurry up and fix this." He said nothing more as he left Max in the attic, alone.

In mock prayer, Max lifted his eyes upward and froze. His pulse increased. His fingers tapped against his thighs.

The attic ceiling had been built from old wooden slats. Max moved in close. Dark marks ran across several of the boards. Letters, parts of words, a name — ILL UNGER'S G — and beneath that — EST 19 — the rest illegible. If these slats had been reclaimed from old buildings, then perhaps Max had found his clue.

As fast as his hands could move, Max whipped out a small notebook and wrote down the letters exactly as they appeared. This meant something, he knew it. He could feel it. Every researching bone in his body shivered with excitement.

He dropped down into the baby's room and hurried outside. *Unger* was clearly a name and *ill* could be *Bill* or *Will* or even *Jill* or possibly a longer, odd first name like *Winthill.* The *G* left open a myriad of possibilities, and he would have to calmly think it over — something his brain could not achieve at that moment. With his keys jangling, he fumbled open the lock to his car.

Before he could open the door, Libby Broward approached. "We may have a serious problem."

Chapter 15

LIBBY CROSSED HER ARMS over her chest as they walked uphill away from the house. Max waited for her to speak. Mostly, he concentrated on not throwing out a sarcastic comment.

Across the street, homes of brick sat on narrow man-made hills. To his right, they walked by a charming white house with gray-blue painted bricks along the bottom. On the right side of the house, an overhang protected a new, silver BMW convertible.

These were homes of average people living their average lives. Some well off, some struggling. A normal neighborhood.

Max had spent plenty of time dealing with ghosts and witches. But most of those homes had been tucked away; most of the horrors had been underground or hiding in the shadows. He glanced back at the Darians' house. It stood amongst the others but wore its charm like a mask.

Libby cleared her throat. "Tell me your opinion of Wayne."

"Now you care about my opinion?"

"I'm not trying to fight with you. I'm asking because we're on the same side. We're both trying to help Wayne and Shawnee."

"Easy there," Max said, for his benefit as much as hers.

Libby's arms tightened around her. "Forgive me for not being in a joking mood. Now tell me what you think of him."

Max thought of the strangeness he had seen in Wayne. "He's definitely troubled."

"I'm afraid of the effect the stress might be having on this couple. That's often how a malicious spirit works — divide and conquer. I've seen the behavior changes in Wayne. I think whatever's attacking them is starting to focus on him more."

"Isn't this thing going after Shawnee's baby? Isn't that what we've all been worried about?"

"There's more than one way to get at something. Right now, Shawnee's on alert. She's actively trying to protect her baby which makes it harder for any kind of malevolence to succeed."

"You think it's going after Wayne now?"

Libby stopped and turned Max by the shoulder to face her. "Not just Wayne. We're all at risk." She scanned up and down the street as if afraid someone might be eavesdropping. "Not that long ago, I made the mistake of dating one of my co-workers. Not any of these guys here. A man named Keith. We were on a case, and maybe it was the pressure or some survival instinct or I-don't-know-what, but we ended up together. There was a full-blown poltergeist in that house, and it came after us bad."

"What do you mean? It physically assaulted you?"

"No. It wormed its way into Keith's head. Confused him until he saw me as the monster. He started accusing me of sleeping around, he grew paranoid — afraid I might try to kill him — and he became overbearing on a daily basis. None of these characteristics were typical of him. Eventually, well ..." Her hand drifted up to her cheek. "He hit me. Right in front of Carl. Which turned out to be a good thing because Carl tackled him. We tried to get him to see what was happening, to get him to leave the case, but he refused. So, we fired him and ultimately, we had to put a restraining order out on him. Being forced away from the house eventually broke the control the poltergeist had on him, but the damage was done. I've never seen him since. The point is that these things can come after us, try to create more strife between us and use that strife to destroy us. I know this is a personal thing to ask, but is everything good between you and your wife?"

Max leveled his best poker face at Libby. "We're fine. We've faced plenty of this kind of thing together. Don't worry about us."

He walked back towards his car, leaving Libby alone. As he

thumped into the driver's seat, he glanced in the rearview mirror and saw her walking further up the neighborhood street.

Driving home, Max's mind flooded with the serious dangers they faced. He could no longer postpone dealing with the pregnancy test he had found in their house. Part of him had hoped to wait until this case had ended. Part of him hoped never to have to deal with anything. But he knew Libby had nailed the head of the problem. If there was any discord between him and Sandra, whatever lived in that house would find it and use it against them.

Later that evening, when Sandra returned home, Max had a candlelit dinner of Wendy's combo meals waiting for her — one hamburger, one chicken sandwich, and one beaming smile. She giggled at the sight, but he sensed the caution hiding behind her eyes.

Dumb move, Max. He had used the candlelit fast food dinner before and this may have been a case of going to the well one-too-many times. Sandra knew something was up.

Still, she played along. "What a thoughtful surprise. I'm famished." She sat at the table and tucked into her French fries.

Max took the chair opposite her feeling like a player in a chess tournament about to face a dreaded opponent. He hated that such a feeling could be attributed to any interaction with his wife but saw no better way to deal with their current problems. He reminded himself there was no need for nerves. This would be a joyful conversation because he would be opening to her that he was ready to do the thing she wanted — to create a baby.

"I hoped we could have a little talk —"

Sandra clicked her nails on the table before washing down a bit of hamburger. "Before we start that, tell me how the case went today. Did you go to the Darians' house? And what happened with Mother Hope?"

Max allowed himself to be deflected into this different conversation. He laid out his meeting with Mother Hope, skillfully glossing over the more treacherous details and skipping entirely the promise he had made. He also neglected the phone call with his mother and jumped straight to the Darians' house. That part of the story he left completely intact.

"So this name, Unger, it was on the wood?"

"Yup. Couldn't have been clearer."

"What's it from? What does it mean?"

"I don't know, but we'll find out. For now, I want to talk about —"

Sandra's body tensed. "Maybe we should put conversations about us on hold until we're finished with this case. This Unger seems like something we need to focus on."

Max watched her eyes, wondering what she could be so scared to talk about. "We have to talk about this — for the case. Whatever is attacking the Darians will try to come between us. It'll sense this unresolved talk, and it'll exploit it."

Sandra lowered her gaze, and her hand rested on her stomach. With a shuddering sigh, she said, "Okay. I've not been trying to hide things from you. I simply needed to be ready first. And you're right. In order to help Shawnee and Wayne, we have to clear things up between us."

"So, there is something between us?"

"Not like that. You know I would tell you any problem I had like that. We've come too far to hold secrets from each other."

"Then what's this all about? I mean, I think I know, and I have an answer that'll make you happy. So why are we both so nervous?"

Reaching across the table, Sandra held Max's hand. She gave him a slight squeeze. "Nothing to fear. I went to the doctor today, so that I could schedule —"

"Max? Sandra?" Drummond's voice blared from down the hall. Max only had enough time to share a look of disappointment with Sandra; however, he swore she looked relieved. Drummond soared in. He circled the ceiling before dropping into the table, settling himself between them.

"I tell you guys, you would never be able to solve a case

without me. It's crazy. You're always relying on me finding these people, and I have done it again. I have found a connection. Without me, you'd still be digging through your books, I'm sure."

Max thumped his back against the chair. "Are you going to keep boasting or are you going to actually tell us something?"

"You wanted a connection, I give you Floyd Johnson."

Chapter 16

DRUMMOND HELD STILL after his triumphant declaration. His eyes fell upon the food and the candlelight and the perturbed gazes directed at him. "Am I interrupting one of your married date things?"

"Yes," Max said, tossing his napkin on the table.

"Sorry about that. I can come back."

Sandra wiped her mouth. "Don't be silly. We can date anytime. This case is much more pressing. So, tell us, who's Floyd Johnson and when do we meet him?"

Drummond bit his bottom lip and rubbed the back of his neck. "I may have misspoken. I don't exactly have Floyd Johnson in hand, but I know he's the man we want."

Pushing back his chair, Max said, "At least, tell us how you know that."

"Floyd Johnson was a former employee of the Casper Company. And though he didn't die tragically at the Darian house, he did die tragically."

"Tragically? What happened?"

"I don't know exactly. We can ask him when I find him."

"You don't have the guy, but somehow you know all about him. Except you don't know the key details of what you do know. How does that happen?"

Drummond kicked the back of Max's chair — a reminder that he could still touch the corporeal world. "Just because I'm dead, doesn't mean I don't know my job. I'm a good detective. Part of that means developing a network of contacts and informants. People on the inside and outside of every situation to help me out. You got yourself a network together yet?"

"Well —"

"Exactly. You still got a lot to learn, and it's important you start to do that learning. Get yourself a network of people here in the real world. I've been doing my end of it in the Other, and it's those contacts that have provided us with the information we needed. That's how I found out about Floyd Johnson."

Sandra offered a warm smile. "You've done well, and we appreciate it."

"Doesn't always feel that way."

"I certainly appreciate it."

Max hurried to add, "And I do, too. Wasn't trying to question your abilities."

Mollified, Drummond continued, "Well, all we've got to do is find him now, and we'll get all the details that we can. I'll go back to the Other and see what's what."

Sandra blew him a kiss. "I wish I could give you a hug, too."

As much as a ghost could, Drummond blushed. "For you, Doll, this is hardly trouble. I'll be back as soon as I can." Drummond left.

In the silence that ensued, Max's mouth twitched from side to side. Sandra got up and disposed of the fast food bags and cartons.

"I'm sorry our date got interrupted," she said.

Max shook his head — not because he didn't believe her, though he had seen her relief. Rather, he shook his head at his own thoughts. "None of this is adding up."

"You mean the case?"

"What do we have? A haunted house that we can't find the ghost haunting it. A house built in the 1920s, yet everything about it, like the bottle, comes from decades earlier. Even this Floyd Johnson is a former Casper employee, so how can he possibly be connected to a house that wasn't even built until the guy was very old or, more likely, dead. And now, we have this piece of wood with the name Unger on it, and that could be any number of things."

"I know how frustrated you feel. I feel it, too. But we're going to have to —" Sandra's cell phone rang. Glancing at it, she frowned. "It's Libby."

Max listened to her end of the conversation — the concern in her voice, the subtle gasp, and the dreaded question *What happened?* When she ended the call, Max said, "Shawnee got attacked again, didn't she?"

"Worst one yet."

Sandra tapped on her phone a moment and then handed it to Max. Libby had sent over a photo of Shawnee that made her look like a domestic abuse victim. Blood glistened on her forehead from a gash leading into her hairline. Her nose had swelled and blood dribbled down to her mouth.

Scratching his head, Max stretched his back. "Guess the day's not over. Let's get going."

He paused a moment as he watched the last of their fast food date swept into the trashcan. He knew the pregnancy issue had been swept away as well, but even though they wouldn't get a chance to talk about it all now, he could still be the man Sandra needed. For the moment, that meant helping the Darians. Soon, it would mean being a father — the best he could be.

Sandra's fingers snapped in front of his face. "You there?"

Max grabbed his coat and keys and headed for the car. "Come on. Let's go help the Darians."

Chapter 17

MAX TRAMPED ACROSS THE DARIANS' FRONT LAWN and into the house. The drive over had been filled with tense silence. His thoughts had been consumed with the failed conversation over Wendy's dinner as well as his frustration towards Libby and the Darians. He understood that Wayne and Shawnee couldn't move away, that they had to deal with the problems of this house, but that didn't mean they had to stay there and keep getting attacked. They could try to sleep in a hotel, at least.

Max chided himself. Angry thinking wouldn't help the situation. Besides, he had been the one to tell Wayne that they couldn't run from this.

Stepping into the living room, Max's thoughts only strengthened — *the Darians should try to run away.* The place looked ransacked. Every piece of furniture had been upended. Several pillows lay in shredded bundles. Their stuffing covered the torn carpet like snow. Shattered picture frames and a broken lamp littered one corner of the room. A jagged crack marred the flatscreen. Parts of the sensitive and expensive filming equipment breached the far wall like a sculpture intruding upon the room.

"Carl's going to be pissed when he sees that," Max said.

From the kitchen, Libby called out, "We're in here."

Sandra hurried ahead while Max yanked the camera tripod out of the wall. When he joined the rest in the kitchen, he found Shawnee sitting with her head tilted back and holding ice against her face. Libby hovered over her like a stage mother.

Stroking Shawnee's hair, Libby said, "The spirit attacked her while she slept on the couch."

Max said, "Did you call for an ambulance?"

"Are you crazy? That would be the stupidest call. Yes, 911, a mysterious ghost-thing tried to kill my friend."

"Not about the spirit world, but for her and the baby, surely the paramedics could do something."

Shawnee dismissed them with her hand. "I'm fine." But her hand swayed like a walking drunk.

Kneeling before Shawnee, Sandra touched the woman's belly. "Son of a bitch," she said and stormed out of the room.

Max followed in her wake. He had to make sure she didn't act in a rage. Strong emotion was always food for these kinds of things.

Sandra charged up the stairs. Before hitting the top, a forced ripped her backwards. Max had only reached the third step when she came crashing down. He caught her, and they tumbled to the floor, his head banging into the front door.

"Sandra?" Libby called from the kitchen. "You okay?"

"We're fine. Thanks for asking," Max said as they untangled. "Well, it wouldn't be a proper case, if I didn't get beat up a little."

When she didn't react with even a slight chuckle, he worried she might have been seriously injured. Looking upon her, though, he saw nothing physically wrong. However, she stared up the stairwell, face pale, her bottom lip trembling.

He reached out for her but held back. He didn't want to startle her. "What's there? What do you see?"

She shook her head. "Nothing. I still see nothing."

A terrible chill slithered across his skin. He knew that feeling. It happened whenever a ghost touched him. "I can feel it. Can't you?"

Sandra nodded.

"If you can't see it, then what the heck is it?"

She jumped to her feet and dashed for the kitchen. Max followed but he could hear her yelling long before reaching her side.

"Why are you still here?" she cried out. "Pack up your stuff and get out of this house."

As Libby spoke, she pulled out some glasses and filled them with peach schnapps. "I know how frightening it can be in here, but understand that first, nothing else has happened here, not like this, until you and Max showed up. Also, I wanted to make sure Shawnee was safe before attempting to move her. But then I realized that without knowing what we're facing here, how can we know anywhere else would be safe?"

"So your answer is what? For all of us to get drunk and try to forget about it?"

"I just wanted to calm things down."

"Calm is not what is called for here. You need a healthy panic. You need to leave this house."

Libby threw back her glass and winced as the alcohol burned its way down her throat. "Have you found anything in your research to suggest that this house has attacked other people? That there's any history in this house?"

Though Sandra knew the answer, she still looked at Max. He could see the wish in her eyes that his answer would be different. He offered the best he could, "Not yet."

"Then it's possible, maybe even likely, that whatever is attacking Shawnee is not connected to the house but to her. Move her and it will follow."

Hearing his own words echoed, Max thought they sounded hollow. They could try, couldn't they? Take Wayne and Shawnee to a hotel and see if they get through the night. They were certainly not safer in the house.

Libby went on, "At least here we have some information and some sense of where it resides strongest — the baby's room. If we go to a different house, an office, anywhere else, we'll be starting over at square one. Do you think Shawnee wants to start over at square one?"

Sandra slammed her hand on the table, and Shawnee jumped. "I think she would prefer to live and have her baby be safe. It doesn't matter what square we're standing on. Maybe if you knew how to do your job better, this wouldn't be happening."

As Libby's face reddened and her mouth tightened, Max

stepped in. "Both of you, stop. Remember discord feeds these kinds of things. You two have got to make nice. For Shawnee's sake."

Shawnee stood and removed the ice from her face. Max knew how bad it must have hurt. He had been punched in the face enough. The bruising would swell more and it would be awhile before she could chew without sharp throbs in her jaw and cheek.

Shawnee clasped Libby's shoulder and Sandra's. "It's my baby, and I say we all go. If this thing follows us, we'll deal with it. But I can't even sleep in here."

Before anyone could argue, Max said, "Great idea. Let's go."

"There's only one thing I need — my back-pillow. It's in my bedroom, and I have to have it."

"Can't we go buy you a new one? Or if we put you in a hotel, I'm sure there will be plenty of pillows."

"Have you ever been pregnant? Anybody in here? Because I can tell you, none of you know what it's like. It hurts, and that pillow is one of the few saving graces I can cling to."

Sandra tried to hide the painful look at Shawnee's words, but Max saw it. Sandra said, "Honey, go get the pillow."

Max did not argue. He wanted to, but he wanted to get out of that house more. Arguing would only delay them, and he would still end up getting the pillow.

Sandra wore her determined, purposeful look. "Now, Honey."

With that, Max found himself climbing the staircase. His nerves jangled as he expected to be rifled back down at any moment. His temples thrummed with the heavy beat of his heart. Each step seemed to add more stairs as he went. He climbed and climbed, wondering if he would be assaulted or shoved or sent into a dark memory, but soon he reached the top and found that only his mind had plagued him.

The hall stretched out before him. All the doors were closed save one — the baby's room. He would have to walk by that open door to reach the master bedroom. His legs refused to move.

"Come on, Max," he whispered. "Get down that hall, grab the pillow, get out of this house."

The way he saw it, he had only two viable options — walk soft and slow, hoping not to disturb anything that might be waiting, or sprint like a madman and get it over with. He deliberated for all of two seconds before pouring every bit of energy into flying down the hall.

He slammed the door open, lost his footing, and met the floor with his face. He rolled to his back and watched as the door shut itself. No — when rolling over, he had kicked it by accident. *Get control of yourself.*

Max crawled up the side of the bed. Once standing, he scanned over the bedroom. No pillow. His eyes fell upon the closed, closet door.

"Why does it always have to be closed?"

With two hesitant steps, he neared the door. Then he recognized his stupid mistake. He had looked everywhere but the bed.

Glancing back, he saw the long pillow designed for a pregnant woman. Relief rushed through his body. A shaking laugh fell from his lips. He reached forward. The pillow felt inviting, and as he thrust it over his shoulder, the room lost its sense of foreboding. He marveled at how powerful the human imagination could be.

That's when he heard the screams from below.

Max's throat constricted as he leaped over the bed. His foot caught the edge of the mattress and he tripped to the floor. Without pause, he popped back to his feet. Wrenching the door open, he heard another scream.

He tore through the hallway, pivoted around the banister, and raced down the stairs, taking them two and three at a time. Momentum bounced him against the front door. Shawnee's long pillow took the brunt of the hit, but Max still experienced a sharp pain in his shoulder.

"Stop it!" Libby said from the kitchen.

Max entered the room, huffing as he took in the scene. Sandra and Libby stood against the kitchen counter, trying to meld even further back while Shawnee sat at the table, flinching with every sharp movement by the man at the center — Wayne. He burned fury — red-faced, spit flying, eyes pinpoints of rage.

"You're all a bunch of hypocrites," he bellowed. "Tell me you're here to help but you do nothing. You make it worse. Look at my wife."

He screeched the last word and Shawnee jumped back, keeping her eyes down.

Though her jaw quavered, Libby tried to speak in a soft voice. "Please, Wayne, I know this has been stressful and upsetting —"

"You don't know shit! You promised to fix all this and instead, my wife is being beaten up by what? Ghosts? I'm supposed to believe in ghosts, for crying out loud." Wayne caught sight of Max and refocused his wrath. "You. We brought you in because you were the experts. Well? What the hell do you have to show me?"

Max exhaled slowly, trying to calm the situation by being relaxed. Inside, his stomach spun circles around itself. "We're narrowing it all down. A little more patience and we'll have —"

"Nothing. You've got nothing and you'll have nothing. And all the time my wife is a punching bag for an invisible bogeyman." Wayne grabbed a handful of wires connecting up the monitors. "All your fancy equipment and you can't do shit." He yanked hard. The wires ripped out with a spark.

Shawnee yelped. "Honey, no! We need these people."

"Lot of good they did you." He pushed a monitor onto the floor and the screen cracked. "I want you all out of my house. Take all this crap with you."

Shawnee clutched Wayne's arm but he shoved her aside. "Please, don't do this. I want them to stay. I want them to help."

"I wanted them to help, too. But they're doing nothing but using us. They just want to get it all on film so they can land a deal on tv and become famous. They don't give a crap about us."

Sandra's jaw set firm and Max knew that look too well — she'd had enough of this. With a determined step, she walked towards Max. Wayne put out an arm to block her, but she slapped him in the face. "You ignorant, stupid, little man. Your wife is in trouble here and so is your baby, and you're going to throw a fit because we can't fix it all as fast as you want. Selfish. See how well you do without us. You and your family will be dead before the week is out."

Wayne stared at her and for a second, Max thought his wife had gotten through to the man. But then Wayne's face turned a heavier shade of red. "Get out of my house! Get out before I kill you all!"

He pulled back his hand as if to slap her. He never got the chance. Max plowed his sore shoulder into Wayne's back. The man careened forward, his head narrowly missing the edge of Shawnee's chair.

Shawnee screamed as tears soaked her face. She crouched by her husband, afraid to touch him and equally afraid to abandon him. With her cheeks puffed up both from crying and from the injuries of her earlier attack, she gazed up at Libby. "Go," she said, the words choking on her tears.

Libby shook her head. "I can't leave you here."

"Please. We'll be okay. Just go."

"But —"

"Go!"

Libby blanched but still did not move. Sandra had to take Libby by the arm and tug her to get the shocked woman moving. As they left the kitchen, Max glared one last time at Shawnee. "This won't end here. Whatever's after you won't go away."

"Then don't give up on us." She stroked the back of Wayne's head. He didn't appear to be unconscious, but he had not stirred either. As quiet settled in the room, she whispered her final word. "Please."

Outside, Max joined Sandra and Libby by his car. Libby stared at the house. She shuddered and sniffled, but she had managed to get a better hold over herself than when inside the kitchen.

"We can't walk away," she said. "At least, I can't."

"Don't worry about that," Sandra said. "We're not going anywhere."

"The rotten thing is Wayne's right. What good are we doing? We're failing here. We don't even know what's causing this, let alone how to deal with it."

Sandra rested her eyes upon Max. "Don't worry. See my husband — he's a super-researcher, and he's only had a short time on this so far. You give him a little more time and he's going to find out what this is all about. I promise."

Max didn't like a promise made for him to fulfill when he wasn't the one doing the promising, but Libby looked at him with such hope that he stayed silent.

"Trust me," Sandra went on. "Research is Max's superpower. He'll beat this thing."

They talked for a few more minutes before they saw Wayne peeking out of the window. Not wanting to cause Shawnee any further trouble, Libby walked off to her car. Max and Sandra glared back at Wayne, but they left, too.

As Max drove off, Sandra kissed his cheek. "You do this for me, okay?"

"You have any doubt?"

She smiled. "No."

"Besides, apparently I made a promise."

Chapter 18

MAX AND SANDRA COLLAPSED ON THEIR COUCH. Exhausted bodies and frazzled nerves had taken their tolls. He wanted to put his arm around Sandra's shoulder, but even with his arms at his sides, he could smell his reek. He needed a shower.

Such a pleasure would not be coming anytime soon. Before Sandra could start snoring, he gave her a soft poke in the side. She mumbled.

"Go upstairs and get in bed," he said.

"You're not coming?"

"I've got a superpower to use, remember?"

With her eyes closed, she said, "Then I'll stay up, too. I can help."

"Thanks, but no. One of us needs to be thinking clearly tomorrow and it ain't going to be me."

Sandra required no further cajoling, though she did need a hand to rise from the couch. Once she stumbled upstairs, Max trudged to his study. The thought *I have a study* flashed through his weary mind and he giggled.

"Okay, time to research."

He decided to start over with the basics, but this time, he would focus on an earlier period. Since nothing useful came from when the house had been built, perhaps he could find something during the time of the Casper Company. That blue bottle was their best clue so far — really, the only solid clue they had.

The other worthwhile find was the name Unger, but with nothing more to narrow the search, the Internet would spew out millions of answers for Max to sift through. That would be pointless. No, Max's instincts said following the Casper

Company made the most sense.

After a while, Max had typed up several notes from his searches. Some of his discoveries were odd, such as the man who, in 1908, sued his father-in-law for stealing his wife. There were also two strange fires at the YMCA — one on January 19, 1908 and the next on January 30, 1908. In February 1888, a widely respected man named William Thaw donated a large sum to Yadkin College. Twenty years later, his son committed murder. Apparently, 1908 was a violent year for Winston-Salem.

Violent, but not connected to the Casper Company.

Earlier, in 1902, Winston's reservoir collapsed, sending nearly one million gallons of water rushing across the city. And in 1915, three notorious *blind tigers* were arrested.

That piqued Max's interest. *Blind tiger* was another term for speakeasy. It came from the practice of saloon owners charging customers to see some type of attraction — such as a blind tiger (most likely a large, old cat in a cage). Then, the customers would be served a "complimentary" alcoholic drink. Because Prohibition made the sale, not the consumption, of alcohol illegal, this game circumvented the law. As time went on, the term became synonymous with anybody dealing in alcohol, legal or otherwise, and for Max, it held the most promise to connect with Casper.

However, after a lot of searching, he had to let the lead go. There were simply too many people using the term back then, and even more people used it now. Bars, bands, and old time bandits all adopted the name, and all of them popped up in even the narrowest search.

He came across a series of photos from the 1920s featuring police officers holding bottles of confiscated alcohol and taking axes to wooden kegs. One photo featured a young officer proudly holding a dark bottle over his head. The bottle's distinct design jumped out at once — a Casper bottle. Unfortunately, further research turned up nothing regarding the officer, Jack Robertson.

Scratching his stubble, Max cleared his search bar and

started over. Again. He decided to review the history of the Casper Company, hoping to locate some nugget that he had missed. He started with the name Floyd Johnson, but that turned up nothing useful. He'd have to leave that one to Drummond.

DAY THREE

Sandra tapped the top of his head. Max jolted awake. He could feel the imprint of the keyboard on his cheek.

"Morning," she said. "I've got coffee brewing."

"My angel."

"How late were you up?"

"I don't even remember falling asleep."

"Any luck with the research?"

"No. Do I still get coffee?"

"Of course."

"Good, because I'm going out to the library to tackle this some more." He kissed Sandra's hand. "We will get somewhere with this. Don't worry."

After downing a mug of coffee, Max shucked off his clothes and threw on fresh ones. Twisting his arm through his neck hole, he slathered on some deodorant. He pecked Sandra's cheek and headed out. Fifteen minutes passed before he slapped his forehead.

"I'm such an idiot," he said. His wonderful wife had made him coffee, gently woke him, and quietly helped him get ready. She asked a few questions but mostly stood nearby in silence.

She was waiting for him to bring up the talk that had been interrupted. She finally was ready to open up. And he had blown it.

The sun had set long before Max returned home. His eyes stung and rubbing them only made it worse. He needed a shower, a meal that didn't contain anything deep-fried, and a long sleep. None of those things would be coming his way, however. Not before he told Sandra what he had learned.

He burst into his study, calling for Sandra to join him. As tired as he felt, his mind swirled with excitement. "I did it," he said as Sandra entered. "I found something important."

"I knew you could do it. Tell me."

Max couldn't sit still. He paced around the room, punctuating his words with each step. "Well, I couldn't find anything about that house and what I learned about the time period didn't really help. But then I decided to check out the area — not Winston-Salem in general, but the specific area. Elizabeth Street."

"Don't make me guess. What did you find out?"

"I found out that just two houses up the street, 1824 Elizabeth, there was a huge scandal in 1925. It all started in September when a woman named Grace Renner went on trial for stealing a hat."

"A hat?"

"Yup. Everything I'm going to tell you came to light because of a stupid hat. Now, during the trial, Renner's sister, Mrs. Charles Johnson, is on the stand and refers to complaints regarding dancing and liquor parties being held in her home. This little remark isn't so terrible in itself, but the editor of the Winston-Salem Journal at that time was Santford Martin. This guy was a devout prohibitionist and he takes a major shine to this story. He smells blood."

"But wasn't everybody having little private parties?"

"Yeah, but this one was admitted to in open court. Plus, Mrs. Johnson made reference to 'riding' in a car with two Winston-Salem police officers."

"I take it *riding* is a euphemism."

"You take it correctly. Martin jumps on this story and fast learns that the sisters, Renner and Johnson, are running a brothel out of their house — one that apparently is servicing the police as well. He prints the story on September 20th and the whole storm begins to roll in. It moves fast. On the second day, Sergeant W. M. Cofer is suspended but the Mayor and the

Police Chief decline to comment. On Day Three, Cofer is fired, the sisters leave town, and the brothel's address is published. The entire neighborhood is being tarnished and this is in a time when local reputations meant a lot more than they do today."

"I'm guessing the neighbors did something bad."

"Not bad, but they did act. The women of the neighborhood got together and started pressuring former Mayor James Hanes to get involved. He had always been a good man to them, and they figured he was their best chance for justice since the current Mayor and Police Chief were clearly playing a game of damage control."

"This is like an old version of Heidi Fleiss."

"Exactly. And I think the top dogs were wetting themselves, afraid that one of the sisters kept a little black book. Making it worse for them, the editor, Martin, was milking the story for everything he could. Not only because it sold newspapers, but because it fed his zealotry about prohibition."

Max's enthusiasm had washed away all his tiredness. He could see his energy infecting Sandra as well.

"So what did Hanes do?" she asked.

"Not much he could do. Especially because the case kept bulldozing along. On the fourth day, Martin published a story in which Sergeant Cofer called himself a scapegoat. He states that his visits to the sister's house were all official business. He was there responding to rumors of illegal dances taking place, but he never found evidence of any wrongdoing."

"Did anybody buy that?"

"Doubtful. Meanwhile, the police searched for the AWOL sisters. By Day Five, rumors start flying that upward of eight police officers would be suspended and many city officials might be involved. And here's where things really get interesting — I'm pretty sure Martin had nothing on Day Five. These rumors might simply have been his own desire or some glory-hound feeding him what he wanted to hear. But, on the sixth day, all the high officials close ranks and hush up. Nobody's talking. So, even if Martin had nothing before, he certainly hit a nerve."

"How many of them were going to this whorehouse?"

Max shrugged. "Maybe all of them. I don't know. But the next day, an ex-cop revealed that the police were protecting hidden booze and the day after that, the eighth day, two detectives are fired. By this point, ministers and other prohibitionists are putting pressure on the city using their pulpits as weapons. Day Ten comes along and the police arrest a man named Ogilvie who had the hidden liquor stored at the Westover Golf Club. He's acquitted for lack of evidence. Don't ask — it was a legal maze that stunk of payoffs and corrupt authority. In the end, twelve days after the start of this whole thing, it all fizzles apart. The officials tighten up and many of the quotes that Martin had published could not be substantiated."

"Wait. You mean they got away with it?"

"Other than those who got fired during the scandal, nobody else had to pay."

With the story out, Max flopped in his desk chair and swiveled around as he let Sandra absorb all he had said.

"I'm missing something," she said. "I mean, that was a fascinating story, but what does it have to do with the Darian case."

Summoning all his remaining energy, he confidently knocked his fist on his desk as he said, "I don't know. But it happened two doors up from their house in the exact time period we've been focusing on."

"That's awful thin."

"There's one more thing — Freddie Robertson. He's the son of Jack Robertson. And Jack was one of the police officers involved in this case. I even found a photo of him holding up a bottle of Casper whiskey."

"What makes Freddie so important?"

"Because, hon, he's still alive. We're going to go talk with him tomorrow, and all my researching instincts are telling me that he's going to bring everything together for us."

"I hope you're right," she said, but she looked doubtful. Her furrowed brow did not ease as the conversation ended. If anything, Max thought the wrinkles deepened.

"Something happen today?" he asked.

"Nothing bad. I got a call from Libby. She said things have quieted down. Shawnee called her and said there haven't been any more incidents yet. Wayne still refuses to let Libby back in the house, but so far, so good."

"That's a relief. For now, at least."

Sandra did not appear relieved. Her hands clenched as she seemed to be mounting her strength for something. Max's tired brain finally clicked in — this was it. The conversation they had been dancing around finally had no place to escape.

He could make it easier for her, though. At least, easier to get started. "I found your pregnancy test in the trash."

Sandra gazed at him, her eyes searching for his reaction to this news. "Are you upset?"

"That you hid it from me or that it's negative?"

"I didn't hide it from you. I just wasn't going to talk about it unless there was something to talk about. But it was negative, so what was the point?"

"The point is that you want to get pregnant and that's a big deal for both of us. The point is that just because you've got the womb doesn't mean I'm superfluous in all of this."

Sandra sat back, her frown no longer one of worry. Rather, she looked confused. "What makes you think I want a baby?"

Now, Max looked confused. "I thought ... well, my mother said ..."

"Your mother?"

"You don't want a baby?"

"You talked with your mother about this?"

"I'm not close friends with a lot of people who have had babies. You don't want a baby?"

"No. Not at all."

"But the way you've been acting lately —"

"I'm terrified of getting pregnant. I mean I'm not scared of being pregnant or being a mother or anything like that. My fears are about the kind of person I am, we are, and what that means. Ever since we faced the witch Welling and she possessed me, I've been worried. I refuse to let my body, especially my pregnant body, go through that again. You see what's happening with the Darians. No way will I allow that to happen to me. To us. My body belongs to me and only me."

"But what about the doctor visits? Are you ill?"

Sandra rubbed her face. "Oh, honey, I'm fine. I'm sorry I worried you so much."

"Still worried over here. What's with the doctor?"

"I was looking into getting my tubes tied. If you're okay with it, I want to make it you and me forever. No kids. Just us, fighting the ghosts and holding on to each other."

Max walked around the desk and stood before his wife. His thoughts jumbled with his spinning emotions like a ship flipping in the water as it fell into a whirlpool. He would sort through it all later. For now, his wife needed his assurance that they were fine. And they were. He had his answers, and while part of him had warmed to the idea of fatherhood, his love for Sandra far outweighed any feelings toward a non-existent child.

He sat on Sandra's lap. She let out an *oof* but laughed. "Mrs. Porter, if I weren't so dead tired, I'd take you to the bedroom."

"Well, Mr. Porter, you are dead tired. And you smell worse than a wet dog. So, go shower and get some rest."

They kissed. Max pressed his forehead against hers, looked into her eyes with warmth, and then stood. But before he could reach the door, Marshall Drummond appeared behind the desk.

"Great news," the ghost said and whisked straight through the desk. "I know where we can find Floyd Johnson."

Max perked up. "You've got him?"

"I found him. See, this is where a network of contacts comes in handy. They all came back empty-handed."

Sandra chuckled. "That sure is handy."

"Doll, let me tell you, no news can be very significant. Without a single ghost in the Other finding any hint of Floyd Johnson, that told me he wasn't in the Other. But based on the information I had about him having a tragic death, I thought it wasn't likely he moved on. That and the fact that several of my contacts reported having seen Johnson in the Other previously."

Exhaustion took the better part of Max's patience. "Get to the point."

Drummond dismissed Max's tone as he turned toward Sandra. "Floyd Johnson must have found out someone was looking for him. He's hiding."

Understanding crossed Sandra's face. "He's a ghost that hasn't moved on and doesn't want to go to the Other. He'll be near his grave."

"Exactly," Drummond said and floated backwards with pride.

Max tipped an imaginary hat. "Good work. Now, I'm going to sleep."

"What? We should go out and talk with him."

"Not tonight. I need rest. Plus, I have no desire to face a ghost in the middle of the night. Especially a ghost that's trying to avoid us. And we have an important lead with a guy named Freddie Robertson. Sandra can fill you in, if she wants to stay up. I'll talk with Robertson first thing in the morning and then visit your ghost."

Drummond swished across the room to block the door. "I'm coming with you."

"Sorry. Only Sandra gets to share my bed."

"Cranky-tired and still a smart ass."

"I try."

"I'm coming with you tomorrow."

Before Max could say a word, Sandra interjected, "That's a good idea. I've got a follow up with my doctor, so you should have Drummond along. Don't want you to face any of this alone."

"Yeah, listen to your wife. Besides, how are you going to talk with Floyd Johnson when I'm the only ghost you connect with?"

"Relax," Max said. "I was going to say it was a good idea. Drummond should come along."

A brief pause. Then Drummond said, "Oh. Okay, then. See you in the morning."

Chapter 19

DAY FOUR

THE FOLLOWING MORNING, Max contacted Freddie Robertson. He found the man quite agreeable to a meeting.

"At my age, any company is welcome," Robertson said over the phone.

He suggested they meet at the Geeksboro Cafe, a little place off Battleground Avenue in Greensboro. It was a colorful coffee shop with a massive projector and screen showing old black-and-white movies. Secondhand sofas and reading chairs lined the walls while long tables occupied the main floor space. Several people sat at them and played various board games — most of which Max had never seen before.

"What kind of place is this?" Drummond said as he spied over the shoulder of one player.

"It *is* called Geeksboro Cafe. I'm guessing these are the games geeks like to play." Max glanced at one wall filled with shelves of board games. Titles like Catan, Carcasonne, and Resistance drew his attention.

"This is nuts."

"No nuttier than sports fans that cover themselves in team colors and know every statistic down to the shoe size of every player. These are just people who really like ... whatever these games are. Besides, we're not here to play. We're here to interview a guy."

A voice called from the back. "Max Porter?"

Drummond clicked his tongue. "Guess we found him."

Short and bald, Robertson had the heft of a man who had

regularly worked out in his younger years, but now all that muscle had turned against him — drinking a six-pack or two each day probably sped up matters. Still, for a man in his nineties, Freddie Robertson looked remarkable fit.

He waved them over to a small room in the back. Painted blue, it had game tables as well and another sofa. With the lunch rush not yet in swing — Max had no idea if this place even had a lunch rush — the back room was empty. Perfect for their conversation.

"You have any trouble finding the place?" Robertson asked.

"Not at all."

"Why don't you go get yourself something to drink? I'll wait."

"No, thank you. I'm here to talk with you."

"Well, I need something to drink. I'll be right back."

Robertson walked out, and Drummond uttered a curse. "I feared we might be running into one of these types."

"One of what types?"

"This guy — he might have something tell us, he might not, but I guarantee he's going to string it out as long as possible. He's lonely, and he'll do anything to have this conversation fill up his day."

"He's said two words to us. How do you know this already?"

"What he said, the way he said it, and the fact that he went to go get a drink when, if you look at the table right there, he's got a half-cup of whatever that orange stuff is."

Max glanced at the table and saw the cup. This was one reason Max needed Drummond. The dead detective saw the things that Max's untrained eyes often missed.

"Well, we're here and we need to get something out of this guy. We'll just have to try to make it as fast and direct as possible."

Drummond chuckled. "Good luck."

Max's interrogation techniques, his observation skills, all the things he needed to be a good detective, had improved much since he had met Drummond, but he had hoped the ghost would offer more than *Good luck* when the time came.

Robertson returned, sat, and sipped his coffee a moment. Then before Max could launch his first question, Robertson smiled and said, "So, tell me Mr. Porter, you married?"

"Yes."

"Any children?"

Max knew he paused before saying *No* and he wondered if Drummond or Robertson had noticed.

"Well, if you ever do have children, you make sure to raise them right. Make sure that they're not going to abandon you when you get old. I can tell you, I never thought it to be true. Never bothered much to check out my old man when he was in his last years. Here I am and my kids don't want to have anything to do with me. I feel sad about it. I'm not mad at them. I caused it. But there you have it. Be good to your kids, give them love and support, all that kind of crap."

Max saw an opening and took it. "It's actually your father that we wanted talk with you about."

Robertson's scalp wrinkled as he raised his eyes. "What's my old man got to do with anything?"

"I'm writing an article about a house in Winston-Salem and your father's name came up. Not many people are still alive from that time period, and I thought you might remember something, might be able to help me out."

"Is this about that brothel?"

"How'd you know that?"

Drummond moved in. "Careful, Max. Don't tip your hand."

Robertson sipped his coffee and said, "There ain't that much else that my father's name would've shown up on. He was a good cop, but he never really got involved in any big cases that made the newspapers — except that one."

"I see. Well, yes, I am interested in that house and that story. Not trying to cause any trouble for anybody, mind you."

Robertson's mouth broadened into a smile. "Why would it be any trouble? Unless you think my father was guilty of something."

Max could not read Robertson's tone. It seemed pleasant

enough, but the words had a bite that troubled him. For Drummond's part, the ghost stared hard at Robertson but offered no solutions.

Inspiration struck. "I'm sorry, Mr. Robertson, clearly this was the wrong subject to bring up. I'll be on my way."

As Max stood, Drummond snickered. "Smart move. You keep learning more and more from me."

Sure enough, before Max had fully risen, Robertson said, "No, no, stay. It's no problem. I'd be happy to share the stories."

Max settled back. "What do you remember of that time? Anything about your father?"

"Oh, I didn't see my father much. I was a little kid, and in those days, my father had no time for little kids. He walked his beat, got his paycheck, took care of his family — I'm pretty sure he got plastered every weeknight. But he never hit me. Least not unless I'd done something to deserve it. But I was a pretty good kid, so he didn't have cause to wallop me. He didn't beat my mother, either. So, we did pretty good for that time."

"Did your father ever talk about the incident when you were older?"

"I told you, I never spent much time with the old man. That kind of stuff never really came up."

Max hesitated, flummoxed by Robertson's inability to provide useful information.

"He knows something," Drummond said. "Listen to the way he's answering your questions. He's giving very specific answers, very narrow, and not expounding. He's trying to avoid lying but he's omitting things."

Max reviewed the conversation so far. Robertson seemed content to sit in silence and sip his coffee. Finally, Max said, "You said you had stories to share. If you don't know anything about your father, then what would those stories be about?"

Robertson set down his coffee. "Did I say that?"

"You did. Perhaps they're about your mother. Did she work at the brothel?"

"Do not go insulting a man's mother."

"Oh, I didn't mean *that* kind of work. Maybe she was a maid and cleaned the rooms."

"My mother was an angel and would never set foot in such a place."

Drummond nodded. "I've seen many a Southern man defend his mother, and I can tell you that this man is speaking the truth."

"Then what?" Max asked. "I can't sit here all day."

Robertson watched his twiddling thumbs as he spoke. "Well now, hold on. I do have something that might be of interest to you."

When Robertson failed to talk further, Max prodded, "I'm listening."

The elderly man continued to focus his interest on his fingers. However, Max could see that this time, Robertson wasn't stalling. Rather, his memories flooded over him, and he searched for a way to express whatever caused his mouth to tremble.

At length, he said, "First thing you should understand — back then things were tight for us. The Great Depression hadn't happened yet, but we struggled. Every kid did his or her part to help the family. So, even though I was just a tyke, I had my responsibilities. I joined a group of older boys who mowed lawns, trimmed hedges, stuff like that."

"I take it you did the landscaping for this brothel?"

Robertson scowled. "No, I did not. You need to have some patience, young man. Let me tell the story." To emphasize his point, he took a leisurely sip of his coffee. He set it back down with a soft clink.

Drummond slid in close to Robertson. "Give him time. You can see it on his face. He really wants to tell this story."

Max did as instructed. He exuded serenity as he waited. Drummond was right. Robertson was eager to tell his story.

"Now, there I was, a little kid, mowing lawns, weeding, and such. And it comes that our group got hired to do some homes that were on Elizabeth — same road as this brothel. As boys are wont to do, we got a lot of talking going on. One of the boys, his name was Nico — big Italian fellow — he ran the whole business. There was a home about two doors down from the brothel. The missus, she clearly had an eye for Nico, and whenever we mowed that lawn, she always found reasons to call him inside."

"Sorry to interrupt, but that house — was it a blue house?"

A flicker of something shot across Robertson's face, but it vanished before he spoke again. "Yup. The blue house. Anyway, this woman, she'd take Nico in and do their thing. I was too young, of course, to know what was going on, but he would come out and tell stories and we all learned about the birds and the bees from those tales.

"Here's where the story's going to take a turn that you might be interested in. You see, Nico bragged that this woman, while her husband was away, would take him down into the basement and they'd have their fun in a tunnel. He called it the Tunnel of Love."

"A tunnel?"

"Yup. He said we wouldn't believe what we'd see there because the tunnel led to the brothel."

"Why is there a tunnel from a stranger's house to the brothel?"

Robertson shook his head and shoulders at the same time. "You ain't too smart."

Drummond nodded. "I've got to second that one."

"You see, young man, Prohibition was going on at the time. If you're going to run an illegal operation like a brothel — a place full of music, dancing, and parties going on — then that means lots of alcohol. And you've got to get the alcohol in. Even if there were a bunch of police on the take, you can't just be hauling bathtubs of hooch through the front door. A corrupt cop can only turn a blind eye to so much. Not to mention that, considering all the high-level members of society that were rumored to frequent this particular establishment, those people would need a way to get in and out without being seen. I don't know if you've been around that area, but the houses are awful close together."

Max smirked. "So, they had a deal with the people in the blue house. With all the booze coming in and the people who had to protect their image sneaking through the tunnel, presumably, the owners of the blue house got a payoff. Is that about right?"

"Now you're understanding. Anyway, Nico really wanted to show off all that was going on. Especially after some of the boys started ribbing him and doubting him. So he said next time the lady of the house called him in, he would take her upstairs to the bedroom. Then we would be able to sneak on in, go downstairs to the basement, and check out the Tunnel of Love for ourselves. Who knows? Maybe we'd even get to see what goes on in that brothel. Well, for a bunch of young boys, there was no question we were going. Next week came around, she called Nico in, and we gave him about five minutes before we all tiptoed down to the basement.

"There it was. This low tunnel leading off into the dark with stairs running down. One of the fellows with us, Jimmy, he got cold feet. So, we posted him on the stairs to warn us if Nico and the lady got finished before we were ready. Then me, Felix, and Coco all went down the tunnel. It was a dank place, not well lit, and all brick. On one side, there were shelves full of liquor. All different kinds. I'd never seen so much booze in my life. When we got to the end, we saw a big, metal door with a sliding peephole up top. We had no doubt that on the other side of that door, we'd find a guard. If we didn't know the password, we'd not be getting any further. Had to be careful back in those days when it came to such things.

"Before you ask, we didn't knock, we didn't know any secret word, and I ain't ever been in that brothel. But even with those walls and doors being thick, we could hear enough. We sat there and listened to somebody partaking in the brothel's services." Robertson gazed at the ceiling, his wrinkled mouth twisting as if he had tasted a foul meal. "I had never heard sex before. Based on the performance that woman gave, I had a misconception about what to expect when my first time came around quite a few years later. We did swipe a taste of all the booze. Nasty stuff, but we had a hell of great time getting drunk. Lots of fun. Until Jimmy yelled for us to get out. We ran back outside and tried our best to mow the lawn without throwing up.

"That's really all I got to tell you. Hope that helps you out, answers your questions, and gives you whatever you're looking for. Now, if you'll excuse me, a friend of mine is coming out here to meet me in a few minutes so that we can play some Magic and talk over happier times." He put out his hand and waited for Max to shake it.

As Max rode along the highway back towards Winston-Salem, Drummond floated above the passenger seat and stared. "Something on my face?" Max said. "What do you want?"

"You don't seem satisfied by what we learned."

"You're the big detective. You didn't really buy that whole thing. Didn't it seem like some made-up, little fantasy?"

"In my experience, never underestimate the will of a man trying to get whores and alcohol. Especially a young man."

"Maybe. But something didn't feel right. Besides, Robertson couldn't have been more than eight at the time. Hardly an age to be seeking out whores."

"Depends. Some of us are more masculine than others. I had urges from when I was six."

"Stop right there. I don't want to know about your urges."

"Look, I told you Robertson might be holding back something. But as far as I could tell, he seemed like a nice, old man. I didn't get a sense that he killed anybody or anything like that."

"I'm not saying anything that extreme. I just think there's more to the story."

"There always is. But if you think he's lying, I can go out to this brothel and pass right through the ground. If there's a tunnel, I'll find it."

"No. I'm pretty sure it does exist. Your confirmation of it is important, but we've got something more important to do right now. Your friend Floyd Johnson's waiting for us. We need to talk with him. Maybe what he says will clear things up, save us all a lot of trouble. And I can't have you checking out this tunnel when I need you in order to talk to Floyd Johnson."

"Your wife can talk to Floyd Johnson for you."

Max struggled to keep his face stoic. "Sandra has a few things to take care of today. She'll be with us later, but right now, I need you. You're the experienced detective."

Drummond made no attempt to hide his smile. "That I am. Glad you're finally learning to appreciate me. Let's go."

Chapter 20

DRUMMOND DIRECTED MAX to the Skinner Warehousing Company — an old brick and steel complex situated on the northern side of Winston-Salem. It sat on a hill with a concrete drive wide enough to handle three trucks. Aside from the main building, two more were connected by a rusting, tin overhead walkway. Weeds poked through cracks in the concrete. Bits of the brick walls had been chipped off. Yet fresh paint covered several docking bay doors as well as doors on the fire escape — all painted a garish purple.

As Max pulled up the drive, he saw an open field in his rear view mirror. It looked to be several acres before the city continued on with more warehouses and other industrial buildings.

Max shut off the car but did not get out. He watched the warehouse. "I thought we were going to a cemetery."

"This is where Floyd Johnson was buried. He never got a real grave. He died in the early 1900s. Back then, this was mostly fields. Over time, the city built up and on top of him."

"Please tell me Floyd isn't Native American. This isn't something like an Indian burial ground."

Drummond snickered. "No. Back in those days, lots of people got buried out in the woods or where there weren't many homes. Cheaper than a cemetery."

"You said he died tragically. What happened to him out here?"

"My informants said he died tragically, but nobody could tell me how."

"Then how can they know it was tragic?"

"Because he won't move on, yet he's hiding in the middle of this warehouse. Something bad had to have happened to him."

"Yeah. I suppose. You know, this place looks like it's actively being used. You have a plan for how we're going to get in there and talk to Floyd?"

"We sneak in, of course. I'll go through the wall, unlock a door for you, we go on in. He should be hanging out in the middle of warehouse B, which is filled with boxes, crates, that kind of thing. Long as we keep it mostly quiet, nobody's going to know we're there."

"You've already checked the place out?"

"I'm good at what I do."

"So you keep telling me. Okay, since you've done the reconnaissance, do we have to worry about surveillance cameras or anything like that?"

"As long as the doors are opened from the inside, they don't trip the alarm. If you open them from the outside, you've got about thirty seconds to punch in a code. But I'll be opening the door for you, so there won't be any problem. You're going to be fine."

"Somehow you don't instill me with great confidence."

While Drummond flew through the building, Max scurried up the drive. Cars rolled by on the main road behind him. Though none of the cars stopped, though nobody jumped out and yelled *Hey, what are you doing?* Max still felt as if a giant, neon sign flashed an arrow over him with the word CRIMINAL emblazoned upon its side. He wished he had waited until the night for this excursion, but had he done that, he would have been facing a ghost in the dark. Perhaps this way was better.

Up ahead a side door opened outward. Max's blood paused until he saw Drummond step forward. The ghost held the door and gestured Max in.

"Anytime now," Drummond grunted.

Other than the strain in Drummond's voice, Max saw no sign of the pain the ghost endured. Touching the corporeal world always brought with it burning agony. Max jogged ahead and slid in past the ghost.

When the door closed, only sunlight illuminated the warehouse; however, stacked crates blocked most of the windows, cutting the light further. Dust clouded the little light that managed to break through.

"Stay close so you don't get lost." Drummond floated ahead. Though his pale skin glowed in the darkness, he shed no light on the surroundings. As Max followed his partner deeper into the warehouse, the limited light dimmed even more. Glancing down some pathways, all Max saw was darkness. Without warning, Drummond halted, and Max nearly walked through the ghost.

Drummond put a finger to his lips. "He's right up ahead."

Of course, Max saw nothing. But long ago, he had decided that seeing one ghost was more than enough. Drummond flew over a section of the boxed-in corridor. He dropped down with fists on hips, facing Max. "Floyd Johnson, I get the feeling you're trying to avoid me." Drummond's smarmy face dropped. "He's running Max. Stop him!"

Before Max could point out the idiocy of Drummond's command, he felt ice pass straight through his body, prickling his skin and numbing his teeth — Floyd Johnson had just zipped by. Drummond dashed through a wall of crates. From a distance, Max heard, "This way, Max. Follow me. Follow my voice. I need your help."

Max tore off into the darkness, following every time Drummond cried out his name. He had no clue what he could do to help, but for the moment, he simply followed in a bizarre version of Marco Polo.

"This way, Max, this way! Come on, Floyd. Stop making this so hard. We just want to talk. Max, over here!"

Max sprinted down one corridor and up another — and twice found himself facing a dead end. All the time, Drummond continued to shout his name and that of Floyd Johnson. Max raced back and opted on a different direction, hoping to meet up with Drummond fast. Up ahead, he caught sight of an open crate with a crowbar leaning against it and a black Sharpie balanced on the top edge. The crowbar wouldn't help fighting a ghost. But a Sharpie — that gave Max an idea.

With marker in hand, he ran harder, cutting down one direction than another, until he finally reached Drummond. His partner hovered at the opposite end of a small clearing with a worktable set to the side. From Drummond's pose, Max had a pretty good idea that Floyd Johnson stood in the middle — between them all.

"Come on, pal. We only want to talk," Drummond said.

Max uncapped the marker. He drew a circle on the side of the nearest crate and filled it in with gibberish symbols. "Floyd, that there's a holding sigil. You can ask Drummond how nasty that can be. You can get near this, now, without it causing a lot of pain. But if I have to, I'll put the final mark on it, and you'll be sorry."

Drummond nodded. "You don't want to mess with Max. He's very talented with magic." Drummond's smile disappeared into a cold, hard expression. "Floyd says you may be strong with magic, but you ain't as strong as the Hulls."

Max's throat tightened. He moved a few steps closer. "Let us help you. We promise we'll protect you from the Hulls."

"That's right," Drummond said. "You can trust us. Whatever they got to do with this, we can handle it." Drummond listened for a moment, then continued, "No, no. You can believe me. That there is Max Porter. Now, look at me, Floyd. The Hulls cursed me, but I'm free thanks to that guy. He's not afraid of them. He's stood up to them many times before. But we can't help you if you clam up. We've got to know your side of this, what your involvement is."

Max waited in the ghostly silence as Floyd responded. After a while, Drummond looked straight at Max. "You are not going to believe this."

Chapter 21

ON JUNE 3, 1898, Floyd Johnson considered himself to be one of the luckiest black men alive — he had been hired by The Casper Company to work in their warehouses, helping ship crates of whiskey. Besides being better than any job Floyd had ever had, it got him away from the back-breaking labor of the tobacco fields. For a man whose parents had been plantation slaves, this job meant a promotion to a better life for him, potential to provide for a wife, and possibly even enough money for a child.

Not two months in, he met Milton Hull. *(Max raised an eyebrow. "Another Hull?" Drummond shrugged. "It's Winston-Salem. You'll always hit into the Hulls.")* Milton was a sharp-looking man with slicked hair and a pencil-thin mustache. He moved with confidence like a movie star who knew everyone watched him and wanted to be like him. At the same time, there was a weakness just behind that mustache. A trembling child within him. Whenever he let a glimpse of that truth slip through, he lost all of his swagger for a few seconds.

Floyd had always been a quick-witted fellow, and Milton liked that. He also liked that Floyd would do most of the heavy lifting in the warehouse.

At lunchtime, the two would often share beers on the rooftop. The entire time, Floyd would be nervous and uncomfortable. White people never treated a man like Floyd this way, and if anyone else in the city found out, it could be dangerous — even deadly. However, this particular white man had the name Hull, and that changed a lot in the equation. Floyd knew that the Hulls were good friends to have.

Obviously, Milton was learning from the ground up so that he could be involved in management in the years to come. Though Floyd never saw another Hull, he figured Casper must have struck a deal, either for money or influence, and Milton's employment was part of the deal.

As their lunches became more frequent, Milton opened up more of his life. He revealed that his connection to the Hull family came via a cousin to those in power. No Hulls controlled The Casper Company. Milton had applied for the job on his own. He planned to learn the whiskey business so that he could start his own company sometime down the road.

"See here, Floyd," Milton said, smoothing down his mustache. "The Hull family, they like the male bloodline. And I'm a cousin through my mother. You understand? My last name — it ain't even really Hull. It's Smalls. So, the main family probably ain't too happy with me using their name. I say screw 'em. I'm learning the whiskey trade fast, and when I can, I'm going to break away from this joint and start my own whiskey trade. And I want you to come with me."

It wasn't until 1900 that Milton found his opportunity. All during those two years, he worked on Floyd and when the time came, he had convinced Floyd to join. For Floyd, the decision was monumental. Giving up a job that had provided him much — only three months earlier, he had married Priscilla Kumsar, and they hoped to have a baby soon. Not that that made for the best time to leave, but Milton promised great success and a higher position — running the entire warehouse. That was more than Floyd ever imagined achieving in his life, so he grabbed the opportunity.

Milton never revealed his full plan until they both had quit — an unpleasant affair but with the result that The Casper Company promised they would never work in the whiskey business again. That first night, as they operated their still in the woods north of downtown Winston-Salem, Milton produced a crate full of empty, blue Casper bottles. He then explained that magic — witchcraft — was a real thing. The Hull family had access to witches, and though Milton's low standing in the family prevented him from directly using these magical women, he had certainly learned a lot from them over the years. He knew a spell or two.

Using witch's magic, he planned to infuse the Casper bottles with a spell that would make their backwoods swill taste better than all others. They would call it the Casper Special to piggyback sales right off those jerks who had tried to screw him over.

Floyd's parents had raised him with a strong religious background. Talks of magic spells and witchcraft scared him worse than the threat of white-hooded men burning down his house in the middle of the night. (*"It was right then, I knew I was working for the Devil," Floyd told Max and Drummond.*) He thought about backing out, leaving Milton and his scheme, but where could he go?

He had a wife and soon a child. The only skill he had was working in the whiskey trade which the Casper folk promised he would never do again. The only other option that remained involved long, hot sweaty days in a backbreaking tobacco field. Not wanting even to contemplate that life, he stayed with Milton Hull, convincing himself that he could maintain the balancing act between keeping a job and keeping his distance from the Devil.

For two years, they succeeded in their endeavor. Casper Special sold well and the Casper Company never found out. Mostly because Prohibition made it easy to keep such things secret. Only select blind tigers knew about Floyd and Milton's company, and they knew only to deal with Floyd. Besides, everybody made so much money off this magic booze, they didn't want to cause problems. (*Max pointed out Prohibition was still a few years away in North Carolina, but Floyd explained that while the laws had not changed things yet, the dry chill of the Prohibitionists had already entered the state. The blind tigers wouldn't get their moniker for years still, but that's how Floyd thought of them.*)

As the year progressed, Floyd noticed that these spells Milton cast did more than simply alter the harsh taste of their whiskey. Milton tried to use magic to manipulate people —

everybody from women to bartenders to distributors — but he lacked the skill of a trained witch. Some who drank from the bottles went insane and killed themselves. Some attacked others. In fact, Milton died trying to cast magic on the bottles.

Chapter 22

FLOYD'S DEMEANOR DARKENED. "That's all I've got to say. Now, let me go."

Max checked with Drummond, and upon receiving an affirmative nod, he scribbled over his fake sigil. Floyd wasted no time. He vanished.

Drummond patted his chest. "Didn't I tell you I'd get you somewhere with this case?"

"I'll hand it to you. You came through. Now, how about you help me find my way out of this place?"

Twenty minutes later, Max sat behind his office desk while Drummond floated near the bookshelves. Sandra had returned and lay on the couch. Max relayed all they had learned.

"And that," Drummond said, "is why you folks need a guy like me. We detectives know how to get the real scoop."

"Okay, Mr. Brilliant Detective," Max said, "how do you solve the glaring gap in all of this?"

"What gap? Floyd Johnson gave up everything you need."

Sandra rested her arm across her forehead. "Uh-oh. Looks like Mr. Brilliant Detective may have missed something."

Drummond squinted at them — a threat that amused Max. "No fair with the two of you ganging up on me. Tell me what this gap is all about."

"Okay, okay. Max and I are going to have to buy you some panties, so you can twist them."

"I don't even know what that means."

Max tapped a pen against his chin as he spoke, "When you

two are done playing, here's the problem. With your worthy addition of Floyd Johnson's information, we now know all about the Casper Company and its illegal offshoot created by Hull and Johnson."

"And we also know," Sandra said, "about this house of scandal two doors up from the Darian home. That place is supposedly connected by a secret tunnel."

"The problem is that there's a good twenty year gap between the two. The house didn't exist when Hull's magic whiskey was being made. So how do they connect?"

Drummond clapped his hands once. "That's easy. The blue bottle."

"Yes and no. First off, the bottle we recovered could be any Casper bottle, not necessarily one that came from Milton Hull."

"Not true. Sandra said she could feel magic coming off that thing."

"Yeah, but could a little bottle have enough magic to cause what we've been seeing at the Darians' house? Magic that's designed simply to make people want to drink more?"

"Don't forget Floyd said it was causing people to go crazy." Drummond held up a finger to pause Max's next comment. He leaned his ear towards his pocket. As he conferred with Leed, Max looked to Sandra, hoping she might be able to hear what was being said. She threw her hands up and shrugged.

"Okay, I got it," Drummond said to his pocket. To Sandra and Max, he went on, "Leed here says that we should stop looking for a haunting. None of what we've been talking about would birth a ghost angry enough to cause what's happening."

Max tossed his pen onto the table. "Isn't that what I just said?"

"You're missing the final point. All these things don't add up, ergo, there is no ghost."

"Ergo?"

"It's Leed's word."

Sandra shot to her feet. "What if Milton Hull infused himself into the bottle?"

Max agreed. "Then he would be the ghost that we're looking

for."

Drummond listened to Leed again, then shook his head. "Leed says that's a nice hypothesis, but remember the bottle was not in the house when Shawnee Darian was most recently attacked. The question Leed has — and frankly, I got it, too — is that if it's not a ghost or spirit or such in the bottle, then what's in there? What's causing all this to happen to the house?"

Sandra slumped back into the couch. "Then we're back at the beginning. We don't know anything."

"Maybe not," Max said. He closed his eyes and tried to hear his recent conversations. "Floyd Johnson mentioned people going insane from the bottle."

Drummond drifted in closer with Max's shift in tone. "Yeah, I already said he said that."

"And we met Freddie Robertson, the cop's son, who also talked about that bottle. In fact, we have a picture of Robertson's father holding one of those blue bottles."

"That's right. And when we interviewed Freddie Robertson, I got the definite sense that he was holding back."

"Perhaps he knows what's in that gap in time."

"You might be right about that. But even if you're not, my gut tells me that fellow knows a lot more than he's told us."

"Then it looks like we need to have another chat with Freddie."

Max and Drummond headed toward the door as Sandra stood. "I'm coming, too," she said.

The corner of Max's mouth rose. "Glad to hear it." He put his arm around her shoulder as they opened the office door.

They didn't get far.

Mother Hope and Leon Moore stood in the doorway. Neither looked welcoming. Leon stepped forward, using his bulk to push Max and Sandra back. Mother Hope entered. Though old and small, she commanded the room through strength of will.

Pointing one crooked finger at Max, she said, "You broke your promise."

Chapter 23

WHENEVER FORCED TO VISIT HIS GRANDMOTHER, Max knew fear absent reason. She had been a shriveled relic, always. Even early photos of her depicted a stark, small, dusty thing. Her voice creaked. Her bad eye had a milky cloud inside, and her good eye sparkled with glints of light he could not find. When Max's mother read him bedtime stories involving evil witches, he always pictured his grandmother. She terrified him.

Mother Hope made Max's grandmother a charming, demure lady.

Without realizing it, Max had stepped deeper into the office. He saw that old witch transform before his eyes. Her glares burned through the air. He kept expecting the walls to ignite.

Drummond watched from the ceiling. "Tell me she's lying. You didn't really promise this witch anything, did you?"

When Max failed to answer, Sandra slapped his cheek. "Answer him. Did you really promise this woman something?"

"He most certainly did," Mother Hope said.

Over her shoulder, Sandra said, "I'm not talking to you."

Max's throat constricted, but he managed a weak sound. "I-I'm sorry." To Mother Hope he added, "I made a promise to the Darians, to help them, and that came first."

"Doesn't work like that. We don't get in line on promises." Mother Hope snapped her fingers and Leon moved in close.

"Sorry about this," Leon said. "But you shouldn't have broken your word."

Though he still had a limp, though he still had a bend in his back, the man hauled back and swung his fist into Max's jaw with serious force. Sandra tried to get between them, but Leon clocked her once in the gut. She fell to the floor as he wrapped his hand around Max's neck and tossed him against the big desk.

Over Leon's shoulder, Max saw Drummond racing down to help. He wanted to crack a smile, but the pain in his jaw kept his mouth closed. It wouldn't have lasted long anyway. As Drummond swooped in, Mother Hope put out her hand and mumbled some words. Though she could not see Drummond, at least Max thought she couldn't, she knew the ghost had to be close by. She clenched her hand, and Drummond slammed into an unseen field.

"She's got a protecting ward around you guys," he said.

Back on her feet, Sandra charged Leon and popped him in the chest. He absorbed the hit and shoved her back to the floor. "Please," he said, "don't make me hurt you."

Leon pivoted back to Max and his fist chopped in again. Max ducked and knocked forward with an uppercut. He clipped Leon, but not enough to cause real damage. Another blow from the man landed in Max's stomach. And another. He had always seen Leon as a meek, old librarian and an aid to Mother Hope. Never as muscle.

But Leon's muscles were plenty strong. Regardless of whether his strength came naturally or if he had assistance from Mother Hope's magic, each blow landed firm. Max dropped to the floor, covering his head. Thankfully, Mother Hope only allowed a few more strikes. Then she grunted a word and Leon backed away.

From the floor, Max watched as a younger woman entered the office. She wore high-heels strapped up her legs. Her firm gait created a distinctive *click-clack* sound.

"Take care of this," Mother Hope said.

The high-heels *click-clacked* to Sandra's desk. Max listened to something — a hammer? — smashing Sandra's laptop. The high-heels then approached Max's desk and the sound of a destroyed computer returned.

"Stop it." Max attempted to rise. Halfway up, he could see Leon moving in.

"Stay down, kid," Drummond said. "They got the upper-hand here. Just let them make their point and leave."

Max raised his hands and settled into a seated position. Sandra had done the same. The woman with the high-heels left before Max could get a look at her, but he guessed that didn't really matter. She had served her purpose and would probably not cross their path again.

Mother Hope's gaze roved around the office. "You've elevated yourself quite well. Last time I was forced to come to you, I recall you occupied an awful-smelling trailer in an equally awful-smelling trailer park. This office must have cost quite a bit, and I imagine you no longer live in squalor. Makes me wonder where all that money came from."

Max had a few sarcastic comments queued up, but a stern look from Sandra kept him quiet.

Sifting through the wrecked computer, Mother Hope said, "The money, the bottle, the case — all things you should have stayed away from. All dangerous. Still, you persist. You're nothing more than a child playing with Papa's loaded gun."

Oh, Max had a good comeback for that, but Drummond's warning glare stopped him.

"Don't you tire of being the Hull's pawn? Yet here you go again — caught up in their lives and meddling with their magic. Don't you ever stop to wonder why they let you do these things?"

Max wanted to say, well, nothing. This time he kept his mouth shut all by himself.

"The bottle you asked me to look into is covered in magic poorly created. The Magi group's archives are quite extensive, particularly regarding the Hull family, so it took little effort to link the bottle with Milton Hull. Your lack of reaction tells me you already know that part. What you most likely do not know is that Milton Hull's weak magical skills did not stop his ambitions. Rarely have I ever seen an object infused with so much dark magic. And because Milton did not cast his spells properly, that bottle is not capable of containing the magic within it. The bottle is worse than a cursed item because its behavior is uncontrolled."

Mother Hope lifted an eyebrow towards Max. When he remained quiet, she looked impressed. "Glad to see you're learning. After I understood the nature of the bottle, I decided to do something a bit risky but worthwhile. I summoned Milton Hull in my office. That's when I saw how terrible the situation truly is. You see, he failed to appear."

"Oh, crap," Sandra said.

"What?" Max asked. "I don't understand. What's that mean?"

Mother Hope squatted in front of Max. "It means that Milton Hull is not entirely dead. Our records suggest that he drowned, but of course, the Hulls keep such matters from public reports. Even his body is buried in the Hull's private cemetery."

"But he's not dead?"

"Three nights from now, my people will sneak onto the property and dig up Milton Hull's casket. They'll salt and burn the body. Then we'll know for sure."

"Why three nights? Why not do it tonight?"

"Because unlike you, I think things through. I won't simply have my people charge in and get caught by the Hulls. In three nights, I'll have all the necessary ingredients to cast a spell that will protect my people from discovery. It's ironic, though, that the only way I could really pull this off is by siphoning the magic from the bottle you provided. Not too much, mind you. I still intend to use the rest for my personal advantage."

She put out her hand, and Leon helped her stand. "Mr. Porter, I made you a promise to provide information about the bottle, and I have fulfilled that promise. You made me a promise that you would not return to the Darian house. You failed to uphold that promise. I have several courses which I could follow. I could curse you. However, that would be a curse upon your wife, as well, and she is blameless in this matter. I could force you out of the state, but again, I would be punishing your wife. In fact, most of what I would like to do to you ends up hurting your wife. Except one thing — I can use you."

Leon bristled but kept his eyes forward.

Mother Hope winked at Max. "Not everybody agrees with my choice." She walked toward the doorway. "Pay attention, Mr. Porter. This is the last warning you'll ever receive. The Darians are a lost cause, now. When the connection to the Hull family was uncovered, the Hulls became the only worthy target. This is no longer your concern. We've got the bottle, we've got the information, and we'll take care of Milton Hull and strike a small blow against the Hull family."

Leon held the door until Mother Hope exited. As he backed out of the office, he offered Sandra a humbling bow. "My sincere apologies for this unpleasantness."

"Wait," Max said. "How is any of this *using* me?"

Mother Hope chuckled. "Oh, I didn't say I'd use you now, for this. But I will call upon you someday."

Leon closed the door.

Nobody moved as the tension settled. At length, Max hauled himself up and offered his wife a hand.

"I ought to smack you again," she said. "You should know better than to promise a witch anything."

Rubbing his sore jaw, Max said, "Sometimes I think that old crone is worse than the Hulls."

"Lower your voice," Drummond said, finally able to come in close now that Mother Hope had left the office. "They're still in the building."

"So? You worried she's fooled herself that we actually like her?"

With a dismayed sigh, Sandra swept the pieces of her laptop into the trash. "Doesn't really matter. I mean, we're still going ahead, right?"

Max wanted to plant a big kiss on his wife. "You're damn right. But we'll have to be a little more cautious in the future."

"A little?"

"Okay, a lot. Still, we're going to have to move fast. She said she was going on the offensive in three days. I don't really care what she does to the Hulls, might even help us in the long run, but none of her plans involve saving the Darians."

"Yeah," Drummond said. "If the Magi group attacks the Hulls, the Darians will suffer for it. That bottle of Milton Hull's is going to connect them into this whole mess."

Sandra said, "So, we've got to work harder."

Drummond brought the brim of his hat down, but Max could still see the smile crawling off his lips. "Okay, you two. If we're going through with this, then we better get to Freddie Robertson before Mother Hope makes him disappear."

"You think she'd do that?"

"He's the only person even remotely connected to any of this that's still alive."

Max grabbed his coat. He didn't have to wait for Sandra and Drummond. They were right behind.

Chapter 24

MAX PRESSED DOWN ON THE ACCELERATOR, zipping along Route 40, weaving through the traffic as he raced towards Greensboro. "Keep an eye out for cops. I'm going as fast as I can."

"How am I going to do that and find Freddie's address at the same time?" Sandra hunched over her cell phone and tapped away. While the name Fred Robertson was common enough in North Carolina, there wouldn't be that many who were also ninety-some years old and living in Greensboro.

"I was talking to Drummond."

Drummond floated in the backseat. "Don't hold back. Go faster."

"I am."

"You can go faster than this. Mother Hope's got her whole organization based in Greensboro. With a phone call, she could have somebody after Robertson before we get halfway there."

Max cut off an eighteen-wheeler in the right lane and received a blaring horn in response. "We're almost halfway to Greensboro, now. Can't you go ahead and check that everything is okay?"

"Of course, I can. Once we've got the address. Plus, I wanted to make sure you both were okay and doing the right thing."

"Got it," Sandra said, showing Drummond the address. "He lives on Lawrence Street. Just off Randleman Road on the south side."

"Thanks, Doll. I'll go take care of that. Be back soon." Drummond disappeared.

Five minutes later, he snapped back into the car. Both Sandra and Max jolted.

Sandra whipped her head back. "Do you have to do it like that?"

"Time is of the essence. I'll be subtle when we're not trying to save a life."

"Save a life? Did they get to him already?"

"Not yet. I didn't see them anywhere nearby. It's possible Mother Hope is keeping the whole thing quiet — even from her own people. I don't know why, though."

As they neared the edge of Greensboro, Max said, "I suspect she doesn't want them knowing she's been siphoning magic off that Casper bottle."

"Whatever it is, it's buying us time. But not much. Ol' Freddie is looking in bad shape."

Max exited onto Randleman Road, drove a few minutes until he reached Lawrence Street, and pulled in. Sandra pointed out the house, and Max screeched to a halt. It was a small, starter home, peeling yellow paint and a half-dead yard. They hustled up to his door and banged loud three times on the wood. "Freddie, open up." To Drummond, Max added, "Would you go in and unlock the door for us?"

Drummond thrust his head through the door. "He's got a dresser barricading it, but I unlocked the door. Good luck."

Max backed up a few steps, ready to charge forward. He'd only done this a few times before, and each time resulted in a sore arm. But as Drummond had pointed out, they didn't have time for subtlety.

He shot forward and slammed into the door. The door slammed back.

Max stumbled to the ground. As Sandra helped him up, he saw that the door had poked slightly ajar — enough to get a foot in. Pressing his face against the opening, he said, "Freddie, come on. Open the door. Don't do anything stupid. We're here to help."

A small voice responded, "There is no helping me."

Max backed up again and charged the door. He launched all

his weight into the air. The dresser knocked back far enough that when he returned to his feet and rubbed his sore arm, they could slip into the house.

"Over here," Drummond said, waving them down a hall.

They entered a small bedroom with family photos on the walls and a cobwebbed ceiling fan hanging askew from above. Old boxes had been dumped on the floor amongst piles of old newspapers, article clippings, and photos — all the memorabilia of a lifetime. Freddie Robertson sat cross-legged on the bed. His head hung low. In front of him, he had placed a .38 Special, a noose, and a bottle of pills.

"Can't decide how to do it," he said. "The gun's heavy in my old hands, and I'm shaking a bit. I might not be able to hold it in the right place and still pull the trigger. A noose — well, I suppose it'd snap my brittle neck well-enough. Except I've always feared drowning, and I think asphyxiating while hanging from a rope seems about as bad. The pills — I don't know if I like the idea of going to sleep and not waking up. I've worried about that happening every night for years. Why should I make my final moments the same?"

Drummond swished in close to Max. "We cannot let this guy off himself."

Max wanted to level his most sarcastic *Really? I'm so thankful to have you here to tell me these things,* but he didn't want to confuse Freddie. Instead, as Sandra bent down to look through one of the boxes, Max moved further in the bedroom and said, "Clearly, you're upset. Let's talk about it."

Freddie wiped the mucous dripping off the tip of his nose, but he never lifted his eyes from his weapons of choice. "Talked enough. It was your talking that brought it all back. Your talking ruined everything."

"I don't understand. Tell me, what was so terrible about our conversation? I can see that it was a scary memory for you, but you didn't mention anything that would warrant killing yourself."

"Get out of here. Leave me alone and never come back. Stop meddling in my life."

Drummond flew behind Freddie. "What you're doing isn't working. We've got to try something a little different. You should threaten to kill him." Drummond raised a hand to hold of Max's reaction. "I'm talking about reverse psychology. The guy says he wants to die, but he hasn't done it because part of him wants to live. So, threaten to kill him, threaten to help him along with suicide, and he'll blubber out everything he knows."

Max did not like that idea. But he had no way to argue with Drummond in front of Freddie — especially an unstable Freddie. He also worried Drummond might try a hard chill on the old guy. It would help saving the guy from suicide, but it would also knock him unconscious, making him useless for information. Mother Hope would gain time, too, to make her move. Plus, at Freddie's age, Max wasn't so sure the guy's body could handle the pain of a ghost's touch.

Sandra rescued them. She gently pushed Max aside and sat on the edge of the bed. "Freddie? Is that your name? I'm Sandra."

"Hi. You're a lovely lady. What're you doing in all this?"

"I'm Max's wife. We're partners in this." She spoke calm and soft. Her tone brought Freddie's eyes up to face her.

"Then I'm sorry, Ma'am, because I can't help you."

"It's not me we're trying to help. There's a woman, a pregnant woman, and her life is in danger. That means her unborn child's life is in danger, too. You understand? We're here not to cause you pain, but because we believe you didn't tell us the whole story you knew. We think that story could help us save her life."

Freddie sniffled loud and rubbed his wet eyes. "I'm sorry. I can't."

"Yes, you can. You're choosing not to."

"I just want to end my pain. That's all."

"Tell me something — have you ever murdered anybody?"

Freddie's mouth dropped open. "Of course not. I'm no monster. I just saw something."

"What did you see?" But Freddie shook his head. Sandra went on, "If you won't talk to us, and you kill yourself, then you will be responsible for the deaths of this woman and her child. And that will make you a murderer. So, you're not only taking your life, you're taking the lives of two others."

"That's not true."

"I know it sucks, but that's the truth. I can't stop you from suicide, but I can offer you this — if you talk with us now, tell us what we need to know, you might save their lives. Isn't that better than taking them?"

Freddie's head swayed to the left and right. Finally, his chin moved up and down in a weak but steady nod. At first his jaw opened, but no sound followed. When he finally spoke, each word seemed to shrink him right before Max's eyes.

"Everything I told you was true up until we were in that tunnel. Me and Coco listened to that closed door, all that moaning, and that's when Felix looked up and found a symbol on the wall."

Max settled next to his wife. "A symbol?"

"You never learn to shut up, do you? You've got to keep your mouth clamped, if you want to hear my story."

Drummond barked out a laugh. "You tell him, Bub." Max startled but if Freddie had noticed, he must have assumed it was in reaction to his own voice.

"I didn't know nothing about symbols back then. But Felix, he knew. He pointed at it and told me it was a witch's symbol. Didn't know what it was for, but he knew that — and it scared him. I think his parents were Romanian or something like that. Guess that's how he knew."

Max wanted to make a comment about racism but held back. At ninety-something years old, Freddie wasn't going to change.

To Sandra, Freddie said, "I'm sorry, ma'am, but if you intend to hear this, you should know that it will get rather impolite."

Sandra warmly rubbed the old man's shoulder. "I think I can handle it."

"I suppose you already know the tunnel led to the brothel. While I sat there looking at this witch's symbol, the sounds of sex got louder. Really loud. It was like it was all around us. My friends, they got scared. Jimmy, the one on the stairs, he panicked and called for us to run. Felix and Coco took off with him, but I stayed. In order for you to understand, I have to say some very indelicate things. See, I stayed because I liked those sounds. Of course, I did. I was a young man and what young man wouldn't want to hear those things. But I especially liked it. I became aroused."

Max said, "So? Why is that so horrible?"

"You see these weapons in front of me? You keep interrupting, and I'll use them. I'm old, but I still know how to fire a pistol — aim may not be that good, but that don't matter when the job gets done." Freddie stared at the weapon, his words filtering back through him. His fingers inched forward. But Max didn't have to lunge across to stop the old man. Freddie stopped himself. He turned up a pathetic grin and said, "Where was I?"

"We were talking about —"

"You stay quiet."

Max made a motion of zipping his lips.

"Understand that back then I had never heard sex before. I was too young. But years later, when I lost my virginity, I got to hear sex again. It was completely different. Nothing was the same. I was not stupid enough to think that every woman would sound exactly alike, but surely the sounds should have been close. There should have been some resemblance. But this was completely wrong. It confused me.

"So, I decided to write down what I remembered from that day in the tunnel. Over and over, I would write the same story. Because each time I went through it, I would recall different details. I was only fifteen at the time I started this; otherwise, I would've figured it out. I'm sure you already have. Anyway, it took me time. Going through that day, writing it down, forcing myself to remember. And finally, I saw it all.

"It was the day after we had been in that tunnel. That night my father came home, and he looked shaken. That's not something he often showed. He would hide an emotion like that. But he was blatantly shaken. From the stairs, I listened as he told my mother about a horrible murder. It was in that house. That's what I had heard. Not sex, but murder. And I had gotten off on it."

Freddie paused. When he spoke again, his pitch lowered, and his countenance darkened. "I've never told anybody that. I've kept it buried all this time. But the past, it always returns. You can't outrun it. You can't out-age it. No matter what, it's there. And it knows. It knows me. Every night, it gets into me. Pounding in my head. Telling me what I already know deep in my bones. That I'm a monster."

Tears welled in Freddie's eyes as his hands caressed the noose. Max walked around the room, trying to give the man some space but also inspecting the boxes spread around the floor.

Sniffling, Freddie said, "Yes, I think the noose is the way to go. Least chance of something going wrong at my age."

Max heard Sandra trying to talk Freddie out of suicide, trying to comfort him from his dark memories, but their voices drifted away. His attention had locked in on one particular box. A stack of notebooks had been placed neatly in the box. The one on top had been labeled in clear, precise print — CASPER BLUE.

He picked up the top notebook. "Did you write this?"

Sandra and Freddie stared at Max as if he had walked in on them in a compromising position.

"Way to go, kid," Drummond said. "Here I thought your wife was going to talk that guy out of killing himself."

Once Sandra read the label on the notebook, her expression softened. She asked Freddie, "Did you write that?"

"Oh, yes," Freddie said. "That picture of my father holding up that bottle became famous in my household. Here was his proud moment until the whole scandal. And I wanted to understand because I feared that maybe it was something I had done that night. That somehow, my sin in that tunnel had tarnished my family, and that bottle in his hand was the result. I suppose it was a young boy's mind trying to pull reason out of insanity, but it never quite left me. I became a bit obsessive about it. I'm practically the perfect historian on the subject of The Casper Company."

Max could feel it inside — all the pieces were finding their places. It formed an intuitive leap within him — a sensation he trusted to follow and accept the thoughts that erupted in his head, even if he couldn't grasp his own reasoning. "This is really important. Please let me know — does the name Unger mean anything?"

Freddie nodded. "Sure. Unger General Store. Tragic story, really. What? Why are you looking at me like that?"

Chapter 25

DAY FIVE

MAX AWOKE IN HIS OFFICE CHAIR with a kink in his neck, a book in his hand, and an article on his laptop about Unger's General Store. It had been a long night. When they had returned from Greensboro, Max immediately hit the research books. Sandra had planned to help, but a phone call from Libby changed all that.

Shawnee Darian sat in Libby's apartment, crying and shaken. Unable to deal with the stress of her house, she had left. She hoped Wayne would have joined along, but instead, he pulled a knife on her.

"Something in him, though, stopped it from going further, and I got out of there," she had said.

Sandra could hear Shawnee making excuses between sobs. She left for Libby's place straight away. Max knew that whatever help she could offer, she would. He promised he would find out what Unger's General Store was all about. Drummond even agreed to hit the books with Leed, so Max sent them off with a highly specific research task.

Hours later, as he pored through his original notes, he discovered that he had been sitting on the answer from early on. It had been staring at him the whole time, but he missed it. "Well, I got you now," he said to his notebook.

As the morning light freshened the office — stale coffee being only one of many stale odors in need of freshening — Max stretched his aching body and organized his thoughts. He had the puzzle together now. The story behind the Darians' home led to the story behind Unger's General Store which led to the story behind Floyd Johnson and, to some extent, Milton Hull.

As with all Hull references, the Hull family had done a remarkable job removing their name from every article, entry, book, or paper that he could find. Their thoroughness never ceased to astound. But despite their efforts, Max had managed to piece together the tale. That was why they had hired him years ago — he was one of the best.

Max scratched the coarse stubble on his cheek. That would have to wait a day. He had a plan now — most of a plan — and he would need help. Before he could enact anything, however, he had an important step to take. Shrugging on his coat, Max left the office and went to the corner store for a bagel and coffee.

He walked over a block and up the street. He searched for the young boy — PB, Peanut Butter, Punching Bag, aka the Kid. As he neared their usual spot, his heart sank.

The tarp PB had used for protection from the elements fluttered in tatters. The few possessions PB had kept along the back bricks had been tossed about like the trash scattered about the area. Max's eyes roved for signs of struggle. Thankfully, he saw no blood, but that was small comfort.

He placed the bagel and coffee next to where PB often slept. He stared at it, hoping that his assessment could be wrong, but he knew better — the thugs he had fought with had come back and took their displeasure out on the Kid.

"And I'm responsible."

He should have done more. He could have helped. Only a short while before, he and Sandra had been on the verge of homelessness. Yet all he had done was bring a cheap cup of coffee and a bagel. Not a piece of fruit or a chicken sandwich or juice or anything that might keep a body strong. No, he had opted for the cheap and easy route. With his thoughts clouded, he meandered back to the office.

He stopped at the bank of mail slots. His hands shook badly, and he had to try three times before he could get the key in. Images of PB being beaten to death swirled in his head. He grabbed his mail, slapped shut the little door, and trudged back to his office.

"Man, I had no idea you had such a cushy pad," PB said.

Max stood in his office doorway, his jaw gaping wide open as the Kid spun circles in Max's chair.

"I was just at your place. I thought something had happened to you. I felt terrible. You've been here the whole time?"

"No, man. I was hiding nearby. Watched you and everything. Very nice tears, by the way. I really thought you felt sad for me." PB gestured across to a young, black boy sitting on the couch. "That's my friend. He wants a job, too."

"What?"

"You said if I could find your office, you'd give me a job. What do you think I was hiding for? I didn't know your name, so I couldn't 411 you on the library Internet. So, I waited for you to show up and I followed you here. You bumbled around enough at the mailboxes that I got plenty of time to pick the lock and settle in." He flicked a business card on the table. "Got your name now, too — Max Porter."

Though still in shock, Max smiled. "Oh, you're going to fit in fine here."

"Now, hold on a minute. I ain't heard terms yet. I got to know what we're being paid and what you want us to do. Jammer J here, he ain't even met you until now."

Max arched an eyebrow. "Jammer J?"

"We call him Jam."

"You've got to be kidding me — PB and J?"

Jam answered in a thick, Southern accent. "Hey, are we all gonna sit around and shoot names, or are we gonna talk money?"

"No problem," Max said. "I'll pay you each one hundred and fifty dollars, but you have to do a very specific task, today, exactly as I tell you."

Both boys snapped to attention. PB wiped at his mouth. "Did you say a hundred fifty?"

"Yup. That is if you don't mind breaking a few laws."

The boys grinned.

Max gave them money to buy a cell phone and then told them what he needed. Once PB and J had left the office — Max decided he would call them the Sandwich Boys — he called out for Drummond. It took a few tries, but eventually the ghost appeared. He asked Drummond to get Sandra, Libby, Shawnee, and the others together, and to have them meet at Little Richard's BBQ for lunch.

Drummond frowned. "What about the thing you had Leed and me looking into?"

"Did you find it?"

"No. Looks like somebody took those blueprints a long time ago. But Leed wants to keep trying."

Max paused to think it over. "Forget that. Please, do what I'm asking. Get everyone together. I've got a different tactic to try, and I'll finish it by lunch. I'll meet you all there, and I'll explain everything."

"I like the look in your eye. Don't you worry, I'll get everybody together. Leed won't be happy about it, but I got no problem stopping — if I had to look at one more registry, I'd have lost it. So, what are you going to do?"

"I'm going to visit a brothel."

Max paced the sidewalk, snatching glances up at the brothel house. It was a white building on a short incline with a gray stone retaining wall and similar stone stairs leading up. To the right, an overhang covered the concrete drive, and a BMW had been parked underneath — Max stared at that overhang. He had noticed it before, when walking this street with Libby.

Of course, I saw it. It's only two houses up from the Darians.

But still it struck Max as odd that this particular house had garnered his attention during that walk while others had been ignored. Down the street, the Darians' blue house appeared unoccupied. But Max knew Wayne was in there. He could practically feel the man staring out, watching him like a sniper choosing targets.

"Careful. Don't let your imagination get you."

Wasting the morning on the sidewalk would help no one. Max climbed the stairs and rang the brothel's doorbell.

A woman with a healthy countenance cracked the door open. "May I help you?"

Max attempted his most-easing smile. "Hi. My name's Max, and I'm writing a book on famous homes in the South. Are you aware of the unique history of this place?"

Her cautious stare relaxed. "You mean the brothel?"

"You know?"

"There was an article written recently on it. Would you like to come in and see?" She held the door open wider, and Max entered. He couldn't believe it had been so easy, that the cautious face had become so trusting, which oddly made him feel more cautious. "I'm Denise Williamson. Feel free to look around."

"Thank you, Ms. Williamson."

"Most of the woodwork and moldings are original. Do you know much about the place, yet?"

"Some." On the right, he saw a wooden staircase with a black banister. The risers had been painted white with finished wood on top. It led to a second-floor landing. To the left of the staircase, a hall led to the back, and further left, Max saw a wide open room. It appeared the woman used it as a living room with its large windows and a rather open plan by today's standards — nine foot ceilings, old moldings around every door, a beautiful airy place.

Ms. Williamson stepped into the living room. "I think this was originally the sitting area. Maybe where the girls were put on display."

Max pulled out his phone. "Mind if I take pictures?"

"Be my guest."

As he walked through the house, he felt a strange dichotomy developing between the old and new. In each room, he could feel the nearly-hundred year old occurrences. He could hear the jazz music. He could smell the cigar smoke and flowing whiskey. The pleasurable moans and boisterous laughter — it echoed around him. Yet he also saw modern furniture and decorations, the latest magazines, an ereader, a cell phone, a laptop, a flatscreen, a dishwasher, and a microwave.

As they moved upstairs, he asked the woman about her life. She remained tight-lipped, though she did say that like many in the neighborhood, she worked up the road at the hospital. The upstairs consisted of a narrow hall with rooms attached along the way. Like below, the floors were all polished hardwood. A slight curve near the end led to the master bedroom on the left.

On a king-sized bed, Max noticed an open suitcase and neatly ordered piles of clothing next to it. He paused to stare at the bedroom's ceiling lamp with its ornately-designed molding connecting it all together. "This is a beautiful home."

"Thank you."

Walking back, he glanced through a window into the backyard. It stretched out a small ways with a wooden fence traveling the perimeter. She had a little garden off to the side and a large shed in the back.

"Is that shed original, too?" Max asked.

"I don't think so. If you go in, it certainly doesn't look like it's from the twenties. More like the fifties or sixties, if I had to guess. But I could be wrong."

"Do you mind if I take a look?"

"I'm sorry. I am a bit pressed for time, and I'd have to fish out the key and all."

"It's okay. I don't want to trouble you."

When they reached the front door, she added, "I hope you saw enough. Got what you needed to."

"There is one more thing. If it's okay, I'd like to check out the basement."

"The basement?"

"Yes, if that's okay."

Her cautious eyes returned. At that moment, it might have been dawning upon her that she had admitted a complete stranger into her home based on nothing more than his word. Yet, she led the way to the entrance underneath the stairs. Flicking on a switch, she let him go down the creaking wood stairs. The stairs were simplistic with a single strip of one-by used for a handrail. She did not follow.

Even before he had gone halfway down, the smell of wet earth crept into the air. As he suspected, he found an unfinished basement in the truest sense — dirt floor with an old brick foundation and a low ceiling. It was a narrow, dank, rather creepy place. Duct work hung below, as did loose wires, while pipes went off in different directions. An old wash basin stood in the middle next to a modern water heater, both perched on a brick slab. The basement was lit by a single, bare bulb and two half-covered windows. Black tarps had been used to cover a large number of objects — presumably the things Ms. Williamson wanted to keep dry in this dank section of the house.

Max walked the length of the narrow basement, taking pictures every few steps — far more pictures than he had taken while pretending to be an author upstairs. No matter where he looked, he did not see anything that resembled a door to a tunnel. But there had to be one. If not, if Freddie Robertson had been lying or if he had remembered a different house from somewhere else, then all of this would fail.

"You almost done down there?"

Max took one last picture before returning upstairs. "Sorry if I was taking too long."

Ms. Williamson opened the front door. "Not trying to be rude, but I have a trip ahead of me. I need to finish packing, if I'm going to catch my flight. If you want to come by next week, I'd be happy to let you take your time and really get a good look around. I'll even fish out the key to the shed."

"That would be wonderful."

As he walked down the stone stairs toward his car, Max could feel her eyes on his back — every bit as dark and penetrating as those he felt upon him from the Darian house. He had to drive a full block before he could shake the feeling and think clearly.

He needed that tunnel for the plan to work — no other safe way into the house with Wayne guarding it — and he had already set the Sandwich Boys on their task. The plan was in motion. He had to check himself — was it only his desire, his need, for the tunnel to be there that made him think it was there? No. It had to be there. His gut knew it. Besides, for Sandra and him, the only way ever was through.

As he pulled out of the neighborhood and drove toward the highway, he crossed his fingers. Never before had he relied on his gut with so much riding on that decision. But Drummond believed in such intuitions, and though he would never let the ghost hear it, he had come to respect his partner on such matters.

"Then my gut it is. We'll find that tunnel."

Chapter 26

MAX DELVED INTO HIS BIG, CHOPPED SANDWICH, closed his eyes, and let his tongue enjoy the delicate flavor of the vinegar-based barbecue sauce as it blended with coleslaw and pulled pork to form an exquisite bite. Sandra and Drummond sat next to him. On the opposite side of the table, Libby, Carl, and Jack poked at their lunch.

Little Richard's was busy, as usual, but Max's group managed to push together a few tables and run them parallel to the windows. They left enough room for the waitresses and the other customers to get by, but not by much. The 1950s décor and the constant bustle warmed Max like a comforter in the winter. This place was a good place, and he needed that at the moment.

Max indulged in another mouthful. He knew everybody waited to hear why he had brought them together, but his plan would be dangerous — possibly life-threatening. If he was going to die before another day arrived, he wanted his last meal to be his favorite. As he savored each bite, Sandra explained that Shawnee had left that morning.

"We couldn't keep her," Sandra told Max. "She seemed fine for a few hours, but shortly after sunrise, she said that she had to go back. She had to try to convince Wayne to leave the house with her."

Libby offered vigorous agreement. "Don't think we were going to let her go by herself. We insisted that we tag along to protect her, and she said that would be fine. But then she went into the bathroom, and while we waited, she slipped out the window. We were going to follow her — we assume she went back to the house — but Sandra said we'd only make the situation worse. Wayne doesn't like us very much."

Carl wiped ketchup off his mouth. "It's a good thing you didn't go after her. You ladies would have gotten yourselves killed."

Sandra turned a cold eye upon him. "I think I've faced far worse things than you've ever peed your pants about."

Like a casino dealer ending bets at roulette, Jack waved his hands over the table. "Hey, guys, can we just chill? Stop all this arguing."

"Oh, there's a voice of authority," Drummond said with a snort.

Max cleaned his fingers on a paper napkin and sipped his soda. He sighed with the mixed pleasure and disappointment of swallowing the final bite. "It's okay, everybody. First, we know where Shawnee went. We'll get her back."

Libby snapped her fingers at him. "You don't know that."

"I do. I think I know everything about this case now."

"Well, are you going to enlighten us or would you rather order more food and keep packing it away like there's no tomorrow?"

"That is my fear."

Libby clamped her mouth shut as her ears digested his words.

Max hoped they heard a voice as tough and confident as he tried to sound. Despite his bravado, he found the last bits of his barbecue sandwich binding up in his stomach. He winked at Sandra. In a flash, he saw that she knew the truth. Her hand went onto his knee with a slight squeeze, and her eyes glistened even as she forced on a brave face.

"How bad is this?" she asked.

"At the moment, I'm having fond memories of Dr. Connor."

"That bad?"

Libby blurted in, "Will someone tell us what's going on?"

Drummond said, "Yeah, if you're going to make me sit here and look at all this wonderful food that I can't eat, you better have something to show for it."

Max slid aside his basket of fries before lacing his fingers on the table. He knew how he must have looked, but he wasn't trying to be overly dramatic. Nor was he trying to keep them out of the loop. Rather, he knew once he spoke, once he told them the whole story, everything would move fast. The longer he took to speak, the longer he could cling to this simple, pleasurable moment of having lunch with his wife, his partner, and some fine people who simply wanted to help others. But even as he thought about it, he knew the moment had gone.

"In the late 1800s, Jeremiah Unger opened up a general store here in Winston-Salem. It was on Trade, north of 12th Street, not far from our office. An all-wood building that serviced the entire community in that area. The northern section of the city was not flush with money. In fact, the majority of the populace there were former slaves or the first generation of former slaves struggling to survive in a new world that did not welcome them. But Unger's store did well, and survived for close to a decade.

"This next part, I discovered in my notes from early on but never knew its importance. Turns out, this is the key to everything. On November 2, 1902 at 5:20 in the morning, Winston's reservoir collapsed. Over one million gallons of water thrust down upon that northern section of Winston. Shoddily-made, one-story rental homes of black families were wiped clean from the ground in the flood. Nine people were confirmed dead, but many reports suggested that number had to be a lot higher — the white police officers didn't feel it necessary to count all the black bodies.

"Unger lived above his store along with his wife and two daughters. At first, they must have thought they would survive the flood by holing up on the second story. It could have worked out that way, too, had the surrounding buildings also been multi-story. There might have been enough material blocking the rushing waters to lessen their impact. But Unger's was alone in this way. Couple that with cheap construction and they didn't stand a chance."

With a hand on her chest, Libby said, "So, they drowned?"

"Some. We can hope that's the case. But according to various reports and eyewitness accounts, it appears that the building shattered into pieces. As it washed away, much of Unger's General Store got clogged up against other homes and debris. Unfortunately, screams could be heard for a long time. For some of them, it was a slow, agonizing death."

Max's words hung in the air until Sandra said, "This building, this wood, it was used to build the Darians' house."

Max nodded. "I think the Unger family haunts that wood."

Libby, Carl, and Jack exchanged glances. "That's good news," she said. "That means we know exactly who we're dealing with, and we can help them get to rest."

Max's chair groaned as he shifted. "There's more to this. See, the flood also killed Floyd Johnson and Milton Hull while they were in those woods making whiskey."

"Let me guess," Drummond said. "Their stills were located exactly where Skinner Warehousing now sits."

"It's possible their stills were where we found Floyd's ghost. Or maybe the flood washed him to that location to die. Either way, he has no grave today because nobody found a body — that is, nobody identified his body. Now, this next part I have no proof of, but I suspect that Milton Hull was in the process of making his bottles when he died."

Sandra's face lit up as she connected the dots. "Milton Hull put magic on those bottles to make his horrible whiskey taste better. What if as a last ditch effort to survive, or more likely as a result of his poor magic skills — what if he transferred himself into the bottle? His soul?"

"That's what I'm thinking. And these two events, the Unger's tragic horror being imprinted onto the wood of their building and Milton Hull either willfully or accidentally transferring himself into a bottle, combined in one location — the Darian house. The wood was used to build the house, and Hull's bottles, which by the 1920s were highly sought after, were stored in the tunnel that connected to the brothel. So, the house itself became like a ghost."

Drummond tipped his hat to Max. "I like that. It explains why Sandra and I couldn't find a ghost because it was the house."

Jack appeared to like the idea as well. "The arrival of a baby must have awoken the house."

Libby sat forward. "No. It's worse. The coming baby awoke Milton Hull. That's why the house revealed the bottle." Her eyes widened as she rose to her feet. "The house is trying to protect the Darians because Milton Hull's spirit wants a body. The baby."

Max said, "That's my fear. Wayne is succumbing to Milton Hull's influence. The Hull magic has driven away Wayne's own sanity, but I don't see why Milton doesn't just take over Wayne."

"It's harder. Taking over an adult brain is difficult. The adult will fight back."

Max recalled when a witch had taken over Sandra. In many ways, it was Sandra's fighting spirit that had saved her life. "Then he's after the baby because a baby won't fight back."

"A baby's brain is still developing, and its spirit is completely innocent. Much easier for Milton to step in and take over."

Max gestured for Libby to sit back down. "This is all in line with my thinking, and that's why I have a plan."

Drummond moved around the table, his excitement daring to create warmth around his dead soul. "Max, I like what you've done here. Not only did you put all the pieces together, but you've come with a plan. That's the kind of partner I want. You're making me happy."

Max suppressed a grin. "I think we can defeat this somewhat the same way we would break a binding curse. Except instead of cutting through a circle to break the curse, this curse is in the wood itself. Once the spirits have been let loose from the wood, they can move on and will no longer empower the house."

Carl cleared his throat. "I thought the house was keeping Hull at bay. If you release those spirits, won't he have free reign to do what he wants?"

"Not exactly. He's connected to the bottle that we removed from the house. Now, I gave that bottle to an associate." Max didn't dare call Mother Hope a friend. "That means whatever is still Milton Hull in that house, the part that's attacking Wayne is not complete. I think that as much as the Ungers were using their energy to help the Darians, Milton is able to use that same energy. That's why he was able to attack my wife and Shawnee on different occasions — shaking the house, creating those sounds, and doing all the frightening things he did. There's a battle going on in the foundations of that house between the Ungers and Milton. But Milton is weaker because that bottle is no longer there. Once we have released the Ungers, most of the house's energy will be gone. We can then go to my associate and destroy the bottle. It'll all be over."

Libby smiled. "I don't know if this sounds good or not, but it certainly sounds the best I've heard in a long time. How exactly are we going to let the Unger spirits free?"

"We're going to have to destroy the wood. And since this is magic we're dealing with, we've got to do it in a pure way."

"Purify wood? That's usually done with fire."

"Exactly. We're going to burn the house to the ground."

Chapter 27

MAX DIDN'T LIKE THE PLAN. That it was his plan only made him feel worse. Throughout the remainder of the afternoon, as they discussed the details, he couldn't help but wonder if he had missed something — some small step in this complex affair that would end up getting people hurt. Everybody had a crucial role, and that meant that everybody was vulnerable.

They waited until Ms. Williamson had left her home and night arrived. With the darkness came the danger.

Max had driven down Elizabeth Street several times over the last few hours, watching the homes until he saw that the majority of people had gone to bed. As midnight approached, the streets emptied out. He parked a few doors up from the brothel house.

"You ready?" he asked Sandra.

She pecked him on the cheek. "For luck."

"Don't I get one?" Drummond said from the backseat.

Max forced a chuckle — it sounded as empty as it felt. As they got out of the car, Libby approached from further up. She looked as pale as Drummond. *Good,* Max thought. *Healthy fear might be exactly what she needs.*

Sandra gave Max one more kiss before shifting down the street. She would stand at the Darians' house and wait for his signal. Meanwhile, he and Libby climbed the stone stairs to the front door of the famous brothel.

"I've never done anything like this before," Libby said. "Never broken into somebody's home."

"If it makes you feel any better, we won't be breaking anything. We've got an ace up our sleeve." The door unlocked and Max gently opened it. "It sure helps when you have a ghost on your side."

Libby's eyes roved around, perhaps hoping to see Drummond in some spectral form, but if she spotted anything, she did not react.

"Will you look at this place?" Drummond floated around the brothel, taking in every detail of the ceiling and flooring. "I haven't been in a place like this since I was a young man."

Max's mind filled with a hundred questions, none of which pertained to their current situation. "Please focus," he said. "We've got to find that tunnel."

"Relax. I got this."

But Max couldn't relax. Everything rode on finding that tunnel. If they failed to find the tunnel, or if his instincts were mistaken and there simply was no tunnel, then the whole operation would be a bust — and the two homeless kids he had hired would get the shaft.

Drummond disappeared through the floor. Seconds later, he returned, rubbing his head. "The tunnel is definitely here. I can't get in close. Feels like it's covered in wards. Really hurts."

Though they had now succeeded with step one, Max could hardly be relieved. "No worries. You did your job. We know it's there for real. Libby and I will find a way in."

"I don't mind looking around here some more."

"You can go on a nostalgia trip another time. I need you to talk with Floyd Johnson. He's our insurance policy."

"I know, I know. I'll take care of it." With that, Drummond left the house.

Libby's uneasy laugh echoed in the dark halls. "It's really strange seeing you talk to emptiness. Makes you look a little crazy."

"Maybe I am crazy. Let's get this done." Max checked his watch — ten after midnight.

* * * *

DAY SIX

They didn't have much time left before the Sandwich Boys carried out their assignment. If they didn't find the tunnel by that point, everything would fall apart. Maybe he should have let Drummond stay and help. Except convincing Floyd to aid them would be difficult. Max had to give Drummond as much time as possible for that task. "You take the upstairs. I'll look down here."

Libby gave a short salute, her humor more to ease her nerves than be sarcastic. As Max poked in the rooms, checked doors, knocked on walls, and looked for hidden entrances, part of his mind noted how odd everything sounded. Libby's footfalls upstairs, his own knocks — every sound became hollow and distant in the dark of Ms. Williamson's home.

He had been illegally in places before, but they had been crime scenes or abandoned buildings or businesses. Rarely had he broken into the private residence of an innocent — certainly, not as innocent as Ms. Williamson. This was just some woman's home. Everywhere he looked, he saw the furniture, the photos, the pieces of life that he trespassed. If all went well, she would never know, but that was no comfort. Her touch lay within everything, and he did not relish intruding upon it.

He pushed on, reminding himself of all the people counting on him — especially Shawnee's unborn child.

He entered the kitchen, a narrow but functional room, and caught sight of the green digital display on the stove — 12:15. Only five minutes left. He checked under the sink and in the lower drawers. He removed all the pots and pans to gain access to the back walls but found nothing. His heart quickened even as his stomach sank.

Three more minutes gone and still nothing.

He heard Libby call from upstairs, "I think I found it!"

Max raced up the stairs, two-at-a-time, and bolted around the landing. Libby's shocked face filled his view. Pushing off the wall, he escaped colliding with her.

She stood in front of a thin, door. "Is that what we're looking for?" She opened the door and shined her flashlight on the back wall of the broom closet.

Max followed the beam. A dim, door-shaped outline about chest-high peeked through the painted wall. Max walked right up and kicked hard against the drywall. It crumbled. Cold, dank air puffed out. With his own flashlight, he saw a stone stairwell with an old pipe handrail going down. Above the handrail, painted in white, Max saw a circle with several symbols surrounding it.

"Yeah, this is definitely it."

Sirens rang out. He checked his watch — 12:20. The boys had started their work. The fire department was on its way across town.

Max kicked at the wall. "Shit. We're out of time."

Chapter 28

MAX FLEW DOWN THE STAIRS. Gripping the metal handrail tight, he negotiated the twisting, steep descent until he reached a brick and concrete floor. The researcher in him wanted to stop and examine every detail — the low, arched ceiling made of brick, the wooden shelves stocked with old, half-filled bottles, the rusty lanterns hung from the ceiling, and the repeated wards painted on the walls. But he had no time for such an indulgence. He pulled out his cell and speed-dialed Sandra.

When she answered, he spoke one simple word. "Go."

With Libby safely down, the two stepped through an open metal door and proceeded along the tunnel. About halfway down, they found a metal ladder suspended from the ceiling like the exit out of a sewer. Max aimed his flashlight upward but saw only darkness. "We must be under the house in between. Looks like it's been built over, but I'll bet you, years ago they must have had access to several houses on this block. Makes sense. If your main routes got compromised, you'd still need a way to bring in all the alcohol and VIPs who didn't want to be seen."

Rats squeaked from the darkness. Ignoring the noise, and not wanting to indulge the idea of beady-eyed rodents scurrying around their feet, they pressed onward. At the end of the tunnel, they found a staircase leading up and at the top, a metal door — only waist high and completely flat other than a sliding peephole. And no doorknob.

Max glanced back at Libby. "Okay, this is it."

Though he had seen the fear in her eyes and the slight shake in her knees, her voice sounded firm and in control. "You got it." She hurried back the way they had come.

Max traced the seams of the door. Years of dust caked it like shriveled paint. The cool metal had a slight vibration as if from something mechanical on the other side. Freddie Robertson had never mentioned any of this. But then Max didn't expect a ninety-five-year-old man to remember exactly something from when he was a child — even if he did write about it obsessively. He only remembered the details that mattered to him. Like the sounds.

Max placed his ear against the metal. It was difficult, but he thought he heard a woman's cries. He shook it off, hoping it to be nothing more than his imagination. When he stepped back, the cries continued. They were real — *Shawnee.*

With renewed urgency, Max's fingers retraced the surface of the door. There had to be a way in. Along the top — nothing. Around the peephole — nothing. Along the right side — nothing.

But on the left side, close to his knee, Max discovered a sliding-panel flush in the door. He pushed it back, reached in, and encountered a small hand-grip. He grabbed and yanked back, receiving the satisfying sound of a metal clank.

Max put his shoulder to the door, ignoring the pain from his earlier bruises, and shoved as hard as he could manage. It budged a little but not enough.

Great. Here we go again.

Max moved down two steps. He didn't know if he could generate enough force coming at the door from this angle, but he didn't see any alternative. He shot up and forward, banging into the metal surface. It jerked inward with ease. As he stumbled forward, he found that the door had been hidden behind mounds of clothing next to the washer and dryer. The mechanical vibrations came from the spinning dryer.

Why would Wayne be doing laundry?

Max opened the dryer. His mind yelled at him to leave it alone, but he crouched down and turned his flashlight into the machine. What he found made sense yet turned his stomach at the same time — baby clothes. Wayne was getting ready.

Libby ducked in carrying two canisters of gasoline. Max grabbed them and sent her back for more. From above, he clearly heard Wayne yelling at Sandra.

"I will call the police if you continue to harass me."

Max could not make out Sandra's reply, but he knew she would be calling the man on his bluff.

Wayne's footsteps stomped around for a moment, then even louder, he yelled, "You can't do this."

Max stared at the ceiling and muttered, "Don't push him too hard, hon."

Libby returned with two more gas canisters. After setting them down, she scurried back into the tunnel, and a moment later, she appeared with a crate full of blue Casper bottles. They clanked at different pitches — some were empty; others were filled to varying degrees.

To Max's quizzical look, she said, "They were in the tunnel. I'd hate to see them destroyed. We can use them to prove to the world that magic and ghosts exist."

"You know there's no way I'm taking those out of here."

"Relax. I'm joking," Libby said, but she didn't look too amused. "If I really wanted to take them, I would've gone the other way. I'm giving them to you, so they can go up in the fire with everything else."

Max didn't know whether to believe her or not, but there was no time to argue. He lifted the crate of bottles. While Libby doused the wooden shelves and clothes piles in gasoline, he set the bottles at the top of the stairs.

He could hear Wayne and Sandra arguing, as well as periodic cries that were, no doubt, Shawnee. Max dropped back several stairs and looked at Libby. "Can you handle the rest of this?"

"I've got it. You go do your part."

"When you finish, you make sure to close the tunnel door as well as the one at the brothel. I don't want any of this fire going back up in the other houses."

"I'll take care of it."

"Be safe."

Normally, Max would take a moment for a deep breath, to clear his mind, and possibly count to ten before jumping into any potentially life-threatening situation. But as another fire engine shrieked down a road in the distance, he could not afford such luxuries. He opened the door and stepped into the kitchen.

Little had changed since his previous visit. Wayne had not disposed of the equipment, though much of it remained in disarray from the last scuffle. To Max's left, at the end of the counter, a door led out to the backyard. Max unlocked it, and in came Carl and Jack. All three men stayed quiet as they tiptoed towards the living room.

"You are not coming in here. You are not seeing Shawnee. And you are not welcome — even on my stoop," Wayne bellowed.

"Well, I'm not leaving. You want to threaten about calling the police, again? No? Then all you have to do is let me in. Let me see Shawnee and make sure she's okay."

"I'm her husband, and I'm telling you, she's okay."

"It's after midnight, Wayne. How long you think it'll be until your neighbors call the police for me?"

Max poked his head around the corner. On the opposite side of the room, he saw Wayne filling up the doorway. Max allowed himself a second to marvel at Sandra's strength. That she would stand in front of this bear and continue to find reasons to keep him there, arguing over and over, knowing that at any moment he might snap and attack her — it all made Max love her more.

Other than Carl's equipment, the living room had not been cleaned up from Milton Hull's attack. Along the back wall, Max spied Shawnee. She lay on the couch, sweat soaking her sundress, her legs apart, her face a tight grimace. Another labor pain struck and she moaned while holding her swollen belly. *Crap*. Shawnee delivering her baby now was not part of the plan.

With a wave of his hand, Max motioned to Carl and Jack. Like soldiers on the battlefield, they crouched as they approached Shawnee. She saw them, and Max gestured to keep up the sounds of labor or else she might give them away. Her face trembled out a smile even as her eyes widened with another labor pain wracking her body.

Carl and Jack helped her get up and escorted her towards the back door. Max positioned several feet behind Wayne. He could see Sandra easing back a few steps, giving him room to dash forward and tackle Wayne straight out the door. It would save them both. Once out, the fire would be lit, and they could watch the house burn. All the fires the Sandwich Boys had set would keep the fire department too busy to save this house. It all came together at that moment.

Except Carl's elbow bumped a glass off the kitchen counter. As the shattering sound cut through the air, Wayne whirled around. Though his mouth did not move, the word, *NO!* reverberated throughout the house. The front door shut. Max heard the back door slam shut as well. The blinds screamed down and folded over. Carl, Jack, and Max had one second to exchange looks before each of them lifted off the ground and slammed into the walls. Shawnee screamed out, and Max strained to reach her, to aid her.

The force that held him three feet off the floor smashed his head back into the wall. He felt the drywall give way. And as darkness formed around his eyes, he saw Shawnee rise into the air and float toward Wayne.

Chapter 29

MAX AWOKE WISHING HE HAD A HANGOVER — that would have felt much better than his current state. He gingerly touched a growing lump on the back of his head. Though it hurt, he touched it again.

When he finally opened his eyes, he discovered his body had been thrown into the middle of the living room. No sign of Shawnee. Wayne lay unconscious a few feet away. Carl sat against one wall with his eyes open, though he looked to be in a stupor.

He followed Carl's dead gaze into the kitchen and understood — Jack dangled from above. Shifting slightly, Max saw that Jack's head had gone right through the ceiling — right up to his shoulders. Blood covered his body and pooled a red outline beneath him.

Ignoring the fuzzy waves breaking within his head, Max struggled to his feet. "Carl?" He snapped his fingers. "Carl. You there?"

Carl's breathing turned ragged. "It's real. I mean it's really real. I'd seen stuff before, I'd heard the noises, but nothing like this. This isn't an old house settling. This is a real monster." He cocked his head towards the kitchen. His voice cracked. "Look what it did to Jack."

Max walked over to Wayne while talking. "That's right. This is real. And if you don't want to end up like Jack, you need to get control of yourself." He gave Wayne's shoulder a sharp shove. No reaction.

"Jack was a friend," Carl said, his voice rising in pitch. "I mean we didn't like each other, he was weird and all, but he didn't deserve that."

"None of us deserve that. Now, get up, or we're all going to end up soaking in our own blood. I need your help."

Max tried slapping Wayne's cheek. Still, no response.

His cell phone chirped. Before it finished, Max had answered it. "Sandra."

"Thank goodness you're okay."

"I don't know if okay is the word for it, but I'm alive — which is more than I can say for Jack."

"Damn. What happened in there?"

"I'm guessing Milton Hull's a little ticked off."

"Is Shawnee okay? And the others?"

"They're fine, but not in any shape to help. It's just me."

"Okay. What can we do for you?"

"You can try to get in, but I suspect the doors won't open. Maybe you and Libby can come through the tunnels. I doubt it'll work, though. Milton's got the place on ghost lockdown."

"We'll try anyway."

"If that's no good, the best thing you can do is —" The connection broke. Max looked at the phone — five bars. "Really, Milton, not even a phone call?"

Carl coughed as he rolled onto all fours. "W-Why are you talking with Milton? You working with him?"

"Don't be ridiculous. That bastard is going to pay for all this. And we're going to be fine, Carl."

Carl maneuvered to Wayne. "I'm sure he thought he was going to be fine, but he can't even wake up. And Jack ... Jack ..." He lowered his head to the floor and wept.

A voice, strained tight with pain, wailed from upstairs — Shawnee.

"It's going to be okay." Max didn't know if he offered this to comfort Carl or himself. No comfort came.

He gazed up the stairs. That baby was coming. Premature, but it was coming. And Max had no doubt that Milton caused it all to happen. He needed a body, so he would force one out.

"Not gonna happen." Max stomped up the stairs. Each footfall gaining him strength as his jaw set and his anger flared.

He never saw the punch coming — how could he? — but he felt it. Milton belted Max in the jaw, sending him tumbling down the stairs. The punch hit hard enough, but the stairs did the real damage. The goose egg on the back of his head split open. Blood dribbled down his neck.

Max clambered to his feet and put up his fists. A gut punch came next, strong enough to force him into the middle of the living room. Sputtering air and spit, he avoided stepping on Wayne and Carl as he searched for his opponent.

Nothing.

Finally, Max swung high then low, upper cut, right cross — but he swiped at emptiness.

Something wrapped around Max's ankle and lifted upward. He flipped over before hitting the floor, smashing his face into the wood.

Carl screamed and scampered to the wall. "I want out of here. Get me out of here. Get this to stop. Make it stop."

Max winced as he pushed his body back up. *Carl's losing it, and I'm plain losing.* He patted the back of his head and examined his hand. Not as bad as he thought, but still bleeding. His lip swelled, too, and none of his bones felt firm.

Like a mad genius having a Eureka moment, Carl's crazed glaze sparked with life. "Burn it. That's what we said we should do. We've got to burn it down."

Max tried to respond, but his entire body blasted straight up and banged into the ceiling. He spun like a fan turned on high. Vomit burned up his throat. The power that kept him stuck to the ceiling released. He crashed to the floor.

He rolled onto his back. Everything spun like a drunkard's final moments before unconsciousness. Darkness clouded the edges of his vision.

Except he did not black out. And the darkness had a presence. Mean and ugly and malicious — Milton Hull.

The paint on the ceiling rippled until a pale tendril snaked down to the floor. The thought hit Max that he should move, but the ceiling snake moved first. It sprang forth and wrapped around Max's ankle.

An icy touch slipped over Max's feet and crept up his legs. Like sinking into a winter lake, his legs numbed. When the cold hit his knees, he cried out, his voice only matched by Shawnee's labor cries from upstairs. He tried to sit up but lacked the strength. What little movement he managed received a blow to the chest that thrust him back down. His head lolled to the right.

Carl stared at the snake, whimpering. "We've got to burn it all. That's what we're here to do. Burn it."

With the numbing sensations creeping towards Max's thighs, with his mind numbing as well, the single thought repeated that Milton would kill him as a snake of ceiling paint. Then he heard a gruff and most welcome voice. With the sound, the icy grip released.

"Insurance has arrived." Drummond stood near the front door with one hand in his coat and the other scratching the back of his neck. "Milton, I think you know my friend here, Floyd. He's got a few choice words for you."

Milton recoiled into the ceiling. Max permitted himself two breaths of relief before pushing back onto his feet. The plan had been for Drummond to return with Floyd so that he could talk some sense into Milton — or at least delay Milton long enough for Drummond to apprehend the bastard.

"Easy there, Floyd." Drummond grabbed the air in front of him and wrenched back. "We need this to remain civil. Now, Milty, you've suddenly taken on a bit of a shape there. I'm guessing you're close to transforming into whatever you hope to become. Before you get all upset, why don't the two of you have a calm chat? That would be — oh, crap."

Though Max could not see anything but Drummond, he had no trouble understanding that Floyd and Milton wrestled each other. A lamp shattered. Books flew across the room. A hole appeared in the wall above Carl's head. Carl screamed.

Drummond slid his hat back. "You two couldn't make this easy." He sauntered forward, his fingers curling into fists, and he threw a punch into the air. The wall behind his punch thudded as he hulked in closer. "I can see enough of you now, and I'm going to end this."

Drummond doubled over and soared backwards as Milton tackled him. Drummond blocked an invisible attack with one arm while punching an invisible foe with the other. Max knew his partner could hold his own, but how long was another matter.

Snapping his fingers at Carl, Max said, "We're going to be fine. Get Wayne to safety."

Carl crawled over, but instead of helping Wayne, he shook his head. "We've got a mission." From his pocket, he pulled out a lighter. Mesmerized, he stood and entered the kitchen. He didn't even stop for Jack, but merely stepped around his hanged friend.

Ignoring his pain, Max rushed in to follow. Carl stood at the cellar door with a roll of paper towels in his hand. He lit the roll like a torch.

"Carl, don't."

But Carl tossed the burning roll into the cellar. A loud whoosh scored up into the kitchen along with a bright orange flickering glow. He stared at it for a moment, hypnotized by the dance of flames. Max thought the man might hurl himself into the fire, but instead, Carl turned around and tried to open the backyard door. It wouldn't open. He jammed his elbow into the window. It did not break.

He looked at the growing fire, then at Max. He barreled by Max into the living room. Launching himself into the air, he attempted to cannonball through the front window. An arm of paint snapped out of the wall and swatted him back.

Carl's head drooped. "It won't let us out. We're going to die." He curled into a ball and shuddered.

Drummond appeared to fare better. He had Milton in a headlock (though to Max it looked as if Drummond had his arm looped around air). He bashed Milton's head into the kitchen doorjamb. Before he could utter a smug comment, his head jerked back — Milton must have hit him in the chin. Drummond flailed back.

As he shook off the hit and charged Milton again, Max got

out of the way. If Floyd Johnson remained in the area, he wasn't helping. Drummond was on his own. The dead detective lunged into the wall and disappeared.

Max checked the kitchen. Smoke belched out of the cellar door and rolled along the ceiling. Flames clung to the cabinets.

Panic rose up his throat. Instead of crumbling into a ball like Carl, Max slapped himself in the face. "Clear your head, Max. You still have a plan in action."

A pained roar cracked the air in the house, reverberating through the walls. When Max reached the front of the house, he pivoted and scurried up the stairs, staying low in case Milton managed to strike him. Thankfully, Drummond continued to do a good job of keeping Milton's focus.

Max stepped onto the second floor and went straight for the baby's room. Shawnee would be in there, of course, but he had no idea what else he would find. Part of him hesitated. The rest of him fought on. When he opened the door, however, he froze.

Shawnee floated in the middle of the room, surrounded by a bright, bluish hue. Her legs had been propped up as if in invisible stirrups. Her head and arms hung low. She spun slowly as if laying upon a rotating showroom floor.

She saw him and reached out. "Help me." Her voice barely a whisper yet overflowing with desperation. The sound shot straight through to his bones.

He leaped forward to grab her, but when he came into contact with the bluish hue, electricity arced between it and him. The charge jolted into his skull and reverberated down to his knees. It knocked him off his feet.

He smelled the burning below. Swallowing against his panic, he scanned the room, trying to find the wards that protected Shawnee. But it couldn't be a ward — he was a man, not a ghost. A ward wouldn't stop him from touching her. This had to be some other form of magic.

"Please, help me." Another agonizing labor pain choked off her words.

Max watched her, wanting to help, but his mind went blank.

He stood there, staring at Shawnee like a fool watching television. Tears welled in his eyes, and a dark thought invaded his brain — *Carl's right. We're going to die here.*

Chapter 30

SHAWNEE STARED BACK AT HIM. The plea in her eyes breaking his heart. Except the more she stared, the more Max thought she wasn't looking at him. Rather she looked *through* him. He turned around yet saw nothing in the hallway. That's when Floyd Johnson thrust his ghostly hand into Max's head.

It had been years since Max had suffered such pain. Only once before had a ghost done this to him. And while the worst migraine would have been a delight compared to having a ghost's hand plunged into his skull, it did allow him to see another world.

Floyd stood before him — tall, dark-skinned, strong jaw, and a hint of facial hair, an impressive man cut down at a youthful age. "Bottles," Floyd said.

Max jumped at the sound of the voice and cried out at the extra pain his movement had caused. He couldn't help it. The last time a ghost did this to him, it did not speak.

"Destroy the bottles. Release his hold over this house."

Max dared not move. He stared and endured the pain.

Floyd yelled, "Go." The ghost then withdrew his hand in one fast motion.

Max collapsed, gasping for air. He stumbled forward, getting to his feet as he moved, knowing that any time he had left ran out faster than he could maneuver.

Like a drugged-out teen, he bounced his way down the stairs, rebounding off the handrail and the walls. The single thought — *destroy the bottles* — consumed his aching head.

He entered the living room and immediately dropped to the floor. A thick, gray and black cloud covered the ceiling. Carl had passed out. Max didn't see Drummond anywhere, but he and Milton had to still be fighting. If not, Milton would have killed Max by now. Another roar like thunder rattled the windows and shook the floors — definitely still fighting.

Max crawled on the floor like a new recruit under fire, until he reached Wayne. The coppery taste of blood filled his mouth. He listened to Wayne's chest — heart still beating. He looked across at Carl. Carl's shoulders rose and fell — still breathing.

Max coughed hard. Every time he tried to inhale, he coughed more. The temperature rose steadily. He tried to think, but his mind moved as sluggishly as his body.

He dug his hands underneath Wayne and grunted. He rolled the big man forward. He repeated the actions two more times until Wayne lay next to Carl. Max then crawled towards the couch.

Flames snapped out through the walls and into the living room. Lifting a blanket off of the couch, Max covered his head and breathed in as much air as he could handle. He blitzed into the kitchen.

The heat blasted upon him — a furnace roaring like he imagined the fire and brimstone preachers dreamed of. He knew it would cook his body. Leaping over a burning chair, he reached the top of the cellar stairs. No bottles. They were gone.

The stairs were gone, too. All he could see of the cellar was an inferno as if looking down into Hell itself. Max turned back. Covering his hand with the blanket, he turned on the faucet. Water sizzled out. He soaked the blanket in the sink for as long as he could endure the heat. Not long at all. Mere seconds. He grabbed the wet blanket and dove back into the living room.

With the blanket, he covered Wayne and Carl. It wouldn't be much, but he hoped it would help.

The bottles. They had to be somewhere. A part of him hoped that the flames had already destroyed them. But Milton still had power, Shawnee was still trapped upstairs, and the doors to the house would still not open. If Milton had lost his power, those things would have gone away, and Drummond would have been able to come in and calmly announce that

Milton was no more.

No, the bottles were still in play. Milton had to have removed them at some point, knowing that his vulnerability could be exploited. But where?

Another contraction forced Shawnee's screams. Max glanced up at the ceiling. Milton would put those bottles in the last place to be burned, and the most important room to him at the moment.

Back up the stairs. Only this time, flames consumed the right wall. Smoke fogged the air. Max kept to his belly as he worked his way up.

A loud ringing cut through the crackle of burning wood. He finally recognized it — a fire alarm. It had been going for a long time, but with all the confusion, his mind had never registered it.

When he reached the landing, he watched Drummond pass through a wall into the hallway. Another form followed — Milton. Black smoke curled around his ghostly visage, massive and powerful, as he punched Drummond in the head. He jumped onto Drummond, attempted to strangle him, and shoved him down further. Against such a huge adversary, Max couldn't be sure how much longer his partner would be able to hold out.

Even as Milton held Drummond down, he had the strength to look away, to look at Max. He hissed and thrust out a smoking fist. The swirling black cloud stretched down the hall with all the speed of a jab thrown by a well-trained street fighter. He caught Max on the cheek. A glancing blow off to the side, but it still packed enough power to force Max back a few steps. As Milton wound up for another strike, Drummond reached over and grabbed Milton's neck.

The distraction was enough for an escape. Max sped into the baby's room, but he had to pause a moment. The room was substantially cooler. No smoke. No fire. Whatever magic Milton held, he used a lot of it to protect this newborn he wanted as his vessel. If not for that, Max suspected Milton would have already slaughtered them all. Max inhaled deeply and spewed out black phlegm. Shawnee screamed at him, her pain and fear making her words unintelligible.

"Hang on. I got an idea." He skirted around the blue field and entered the closet.

Pressing his back against the door jamb and his feet on the opposite side, he shimmied upward towards the ceiling. Once high enough, he reached out and shoved open the attic access panel. All of his muscles scolded him as he tried to gain purchase to pull himself further up.

His fingers slipped. He slammed into the floor.

He took a second to wipe blood off his eye before standing again. Though a fiery pain ran along his side, he tried again — shimmied back up, reached out, grabbed the lip of the access hole. This time his fingers caught the lip. He swung over and up, pulling himself into the attic.

The crate of blue Casper bottles sat in the middle of the floor. Max hurried over, snatched one, and smashed it on the wood floor — the same wood that had formed Unger's General Store decades ago.

A howl erupted throughout the house. Louder than the raging flames, louder than the piercing alarms, or the screams of Shawnee's pain. The howl ripped through, shaking the foundations of the building.

From a distance, Max could hear Drummond's voice. "That's it, Max! Do more of whatever you did."

Max grabbed another bottle and shattered it. Another howl. Only this one weaker.

He reached for the whole crate, but the wood floor around it splintered open. Milton's smoke hand poured out. Max stepped back, looking everywhere for a weapon, but dusty boxes of old memorabilia wouldn't stop a pissed-off spirit. The smoke-hand darted at him, snagged his shirt, and yanked him to the side.

It shoved him upward, banging his head into the slanted wood of the roof. Max wondered how many times it had taken for Jack's head to break through the kitchen ceiling. Each blow dazed him, and soon he knew he would learn the answer.

The cold smoke-hand slithered up and around Max's throat. Max tried to shove it away but his hands slipped through the smoke. His head throbbed as if he wore a helmet of bruises beneath his skin. He saw the crate, out of reach, and smelled the charring house drifting into the attic. He thought of Sandra and closed his eyes.

"Quit sleeping on the job," Drummond said, startling Max awake. Drummond crashed through the attic floor. He grabbed Milton's arm and bent it backwards.

Max dropped forward. Coughing and gasping, he went straight for the crate of blue bottles. He picked up the entire crate and tossed it down the access panel onto the baby's closet floor.

The quake that struck felt like a giant had grabbed the house and rocked it from side to side. Max tried to steady himself but he couldn't hold his balance. He toppled over, tumbling into the closet, and onto the blue glass below. He felt shards dig into his back.

Heat and smoke poured into the baby's room. Quivering on the floor, Shawnee held her stomach.

"You did it, Max! You did it!" Drummond hovered overhead, beaming. "Wish you could see this — all of the Unger ghosts are flying away. I can see them. They're saying *Thank you* and man, they look relieved."

Max closed his eyes. He smiled, but he knew it was too late. He had no more strength, he had lost too much blood, his bones were broken — no way could he get out of the house.

"Don't give up on me, Max. I'm telling you. You're going to be okay. The Ungers — they're coming back."

Through a half-closed eye, Max watched as the flames entered the baby's room — Milton Hull's magic no longer protected them. Smoke haloed around the fire. The burning building moved in on Shawnee, but suddenly stopped.

She lifted into the air, only this time there was no fear, no threat — the Ungers were helping. Max lifted up, too. He felt as if he floated on a blow-up cushion in a swimming pool. With Shawnee by his side, the two glided downstairs while the flames formed an orange tunnel. Plenty of air reached their lungs and despite the proximity of the fire, Max felt no heat.

Straight outside, they went. As they were set gently on the grass, Max saw Libby and Sandra helping Wayne and Carl to safety.

With a roar, half the house collapsed in a sparking, fiery blaze. The Fire Department would arrive soon. They would have endless questions.

No matter. The job was done.

Chapter 31

BY THE TIME MAX RECEIVED PERMISSION to join Sandra, Drummond, and Libby in the maternity ward waiting room, he had endured hours of doctors prodding, stitching, and wrapping him up followed by the police asking him questions. A story had been agreed upon ahead of time, and Max stuck to it. He told the officers that they were having a small gathering of friends at the Darian home when the fire broke out. Nice and simple.

The officer pressed a little because of Jack's death, but the body had been burned so severely that Max had no fear of the inquiry turning into a homicide investigation. A nosy detective could certainly discover the numerous oddities, but nobody had a reason to bother. No evidence had survived, and the police had their hands full with a serial arsonist who had set fires all over the city. It became evident that the real concern was dotting *i's* and crossing *t's* for the insurance company.

Soft jazz played in the Forsyth Medical maternity waiting room while newborns cried their first tears down the hall. Every few minutes, Sandra patted Max's knee, assuring herself that he had survived their ordeal. Every few minutes, Drummond crossed through the walls to check on Shawnee's progress and would return with a simple, "Not born yet."

Libby paced the room. Though anxious for the baby, she periodically asked at the desk if they would check on Carl. The nurse patiently explained that Carl had suffered numerous burns and other injuries and would be in surgery for hours more.

To Max's surprise, Wayne had emerged from the fire

unscathed — at least, physically.

Around three in the morning, Max's cell phone chirped — Peanut Butter. "Hey, Ghostman. How'd it all turn out?"

Max kept his face neutral — most expressions aggravated his wounds. "You guys did great. You actually saved people's lives last night."

"By setting fires? You crazy?"

"You really care if I'm crazy or not?"

"Long as you keep paying, we'll keep working."

"You know I can help you — set you up in an apartment or something."

"No, sir. We'll earn our pay and take it from there."

Max had to admire the kid's pluck. Even his pride. "Welcome aboard. Now go get some sleep."

Sleep sounded nice. It would be awhile, though, before they would be home and in bed. And he would want a long shower, too — the smell of burnt wood permeated his skin. Max stretched his legs and opted for a short walk.

He followed Libby down the hall. She turned back and offered a slight smile. "Guess we should count this as a win."

"A big win," Max said.

"Losing Jack doesn't sound like such a great deal. And I doubt Carl's going to want to continue doing this. Looks like I have no team anymore."

"Why don't you join us?" The words had left Max's mouth before he could stop them. Not that he objected, but he knew this was different than the Sandwich Boys. They were guys he would pay from time to time to do odd jobs for him. Somebody like Libby would expect to be an integral part of each case, and for that, he should have given it more thought and discussed it with Sandra.

Libby saved him the trouble. "No, thank you. I like the work, I do, but seeing it go this far — this isn't for me. If I can ever help you in some small ways, I will. You feel free to call me. But I could never do something like this again." She returned to the waiting room, a constant shake in her shoulders. Max wondered if that would ever go away for her.

He walked in the opposite direction and stopped at a soda machine. As he fumbled with a dollar bill, trying to get it crisp enough to be accepted by the machine, he heard a sound that chilled his skin. A distinctive *click-clack* of high-heels.

He looked behind and saw her. More than the heels, he now saw the entire woman — petite, blond, walking away from him. By her coat and the deference given by the nurses, and by her swagger, Max pegged her as a doctor. He followed her. Keeping far enough back to go unnoticed, he watched her turn the corner. As he came around, she headed for the elevators. One set of doors opened at her approach, and she stepped right in.

Max had to decide — get on the elevator with her or let her go and watch what floor she stopped at. Why was this doctor part of the Magi group? Why had she destroyed his computers? Maybe he was wrong. Maybe this was some other high-heeled woman. But that *click-clack* pattern could be no other.

Without realizing it, he had stopped feet away from the elevator. The woman lifted her head and locked eyes with Max. Her lips formed a malicious grin. The doors closed.

Max walked away. He didn't want to be paranoid, but clearly Mother Hope had people all over. Maybe they were worse than the Hulls. Maybe it didn't matter. Hulls, the Magi group — they were all a cancer for everyday people.

Thinking ill of them didn't change matters, though. He had broken his promise to her, and he had destroyed Milton Hull before she could enact her attack on Tucker and the rest of the Hull family. Seeing Ms. High Heels made him think that Mother Hope wouldn't forget about any of it. He would have to be careful.

When he sat next to Sandra in the waiting room, she raised a concerned look. "What's the matter?"

"I'll tell you later. Nothing to do about it now, anyway."

Drummond soared in laughing. "It's done! It's done! Admittedly, premature and the little squirt's got to be taken care of by the doctors and watched carefully, but Shawnee had her baby. Healthy and all is well."

Sandra said, "Well, is it a boy or a girl?"

"No, no. I'm no spoiler. Besides, that's a father's honor. Wayne's coming down the hall now, so you just wait."

Indeed, moments later, Wayne entered the waiting room. Max found it difficult to connect the man he saw with the man who, only hours earlier, had been controlled by an evil force. Now, all that stood before Max and Sandra was a proud father.

"It's a boy," Wayne said.

Everyone rose to their feet to congratulate him and smile and laugh. None of it felt forced. The room filled with genuine care.

Wayne continued, "He's good and healthy. Little but they said he'll be fine. Probably be stuck in here for another month or so, but he'll be okay."

"That's wonderful," Max said. "Does he have name?"

With an odd, sheepish look, Wayne said, "Is your ghost in here?"

Sandra said, "You mean Drummond? Yes, he's here."

"Well, if it's okay with you all, Shawnee and I would like to name our boy Maxwell Drummond Darian."

Drummond's joyful eruption trumped the exultations from the rest of the room.

"I guess that's a *yes*," Wayne said.

Because the baby was premature, Max and Sandra understood they would not get to see him right away. They congratulated Wayne once more and walked to their car. Drummond couldn't be stopped by the staff, so he floated through the walls and spent much of the next day cooing over little Maxwell Drummond.

As Max and Sandra neared their car, he put his arm around her. "We don't always get to win this big. We better savor this one."

Sandra agreed. "I have to ask, though, is this enough for you? Having a baby with your name? It might be the closest you ever get to having a son."

Max took her chin in his hand and gently kissed her lips. "This is all I need or want."

"You sure?"

"Tell you what — let's go home and not make a baby."

They stood in the parking lot, holding each other and gazing into each other's eyes.

Afterword

When I started this series, I thought these Afterword sections would be a chance to jot down a few historical facts about the book and leave it at that. I suspected there would a few readers who found these tidbits interesting and so I kept the whole short and sweet. Well, it turns out that a lot of you folks really like this part. It's one of the top comments I get in fan mail. So, while I still believe in keep an Afterword short, I will endeavor to give you guys a little more this time around.

To start with, let me hit the big points. The brothel on Elizabeth Street and the scandal surrounding it are both real. The Winston-Salem Journal editor who went at this story hard and perhaps fabricated a few details which turned out to scare the higher-ups in this city was a real man. In fact, all the historical details of the scandal are true. Including that the entire thing started because Grace Renner decided to shoplift a hat instead of paying for it, something she should have had no trouble doing when one considers the lucrative business she and her sister ran. However, to the best of my knowledge, there is no tunnel beneath the houses on Elizabeth Street. There is a blue house two doors down, but that's the only real detail about the Darian's home.

Also true is the entire history of the Casper Company, including the way Prohibition destroyed the company. John L. Casper's mysterious behavior toward the end of his life and his eventually demise in Mexico is also true. For those of you who want an even clearer picture of what the blue bottles, google

Casper Whiskey Bottles Images and you should find plenty of Casper Blue bottles to gaze upon.

Finally, the tragedy of the Winston reservoir cracking open and flooding the northern section of the city is also true. There are some startling pictures of the aftermath which show in stark black and white the devastation all that water caused.

Floyd Johnson, Freddie Robertson, and Milton Hull are all fictions of my imagination.

Acknowledgements

Some books require the help of only a few people; some require the help of many. Special thanks this time around go to Alex Matsuro for her books and her help in understanding how real paranormal investigators operate. I took a lot of liberties with the information provided, so for those of you who know about these things, any part of the way Libby and her team operate that seems wrong is my fault alone. Thanks to my Launch Team for all their help and support. Extra thanks to Lisa Gall and Lyn Findlay for their proofreading skills. Also big thanks, huge thanks, a magnificent-sized thanks to Kimberly Gordon for allowing me to walk through her home and take pictures in an attempt to get the details of the brothel correct. This novel quite literally would not have happened without your generosity. And to be clear, the woman that owns the brothel house in this book is in no way meant to be you. Only the house is real, not the characters. Finally, my thanks to my wife and son who make this adventure worthwhile. And, of course, thanks to you folks, my readers. I've said it before, and I mean it: if you keep reading Max Porter books, I'll keep writing them. Without you, none of this really matters.

About the Author

Stuart Jaffe is the author of *The Max Porter Paranormal-Mysteries, The Malja Chronicles,* the *Gillian Boone* novels, *The Bluesman* series, *Real Magic, After The Crash,* and much more. His short stories have appeared in numerous magazines and anthologies. He is the co-host of The Eclectic Review - a weekly podcast about science, art, and well, everything. For those who keep count, the latest animal listing is as follows: one dog, four cats, one albino corn snake, one Brazilian black tarantula, three aquatic turtles, fourteen chickens, and a horse. Thankfully, the chickens and the horse do not live inside the house.

For more information, please visit *www.stuartjaffe.com*

www.ingramcontent.com/pod-product-compliance
Lightning Source LLC
Chambersburg PA
CBHW030520310726
48979CB00010B/1742/J
9781733730877